Camarillo, CA
4/4/11

To: Claudia

May God bless
you always

All-Best
Cynthia

Iceburg

CYNTHIA W. HAMMER

EDITED BY CYNTHIA W. HAMMER AND STEVEN J. HAMMER

authorHOUSE®

AuthorHouse™ LLC
1663 Liberty Drive
Bloomington, IN 47403
www.authorhouse.com
Phone: 1-800-839-8640

This book is a work of fiction. People, places, events, and situations are the product of the author's imagination. Any resemblance to actual persons, living or dead, or historical events, is purely coincidental.

© 2012 Cynthia W. Hammer. All rights reserved.

No part of this book may be reproduced, stored in a retrieval system, or transmitted by any means without the written permission of the author.

Published by AuthorHouse   09/20/2013

ISBN: 978-1-4772-1002-4 (sc)
ISBN: 978-1-4772-1000-0 (hc)
ISBN: 978-1-4772-1001-7 (e)

Library of Congress Control Number: 2012908989

Any people depicted in stock imagery provided by Thinkstock are models, and such images are being used for illustrative purposes only.
Certain stock imagery © Thinkstock.

This book is printed on acid-free paper.

Because of the dynamic nature of the Internet, any web addresses or links contained in this book may have changed since publication and may no longer be valid. The views expressed in this work are solely those of the author and do not necessarily reflect the views of the publisher, and the publisher hereby disclaims any responsibility for them.

Thanks to Rosalie Ballou, Illustrator

I Corinthians 12: 1-11

— Concerning Spiritual Gifts —

This is a story about a little child who dreams the future. Our children are innocent and not yet tainted by the ways of the world. If someone comes to you and says, they have the gift of "sight," don't doubt them, only Believe.

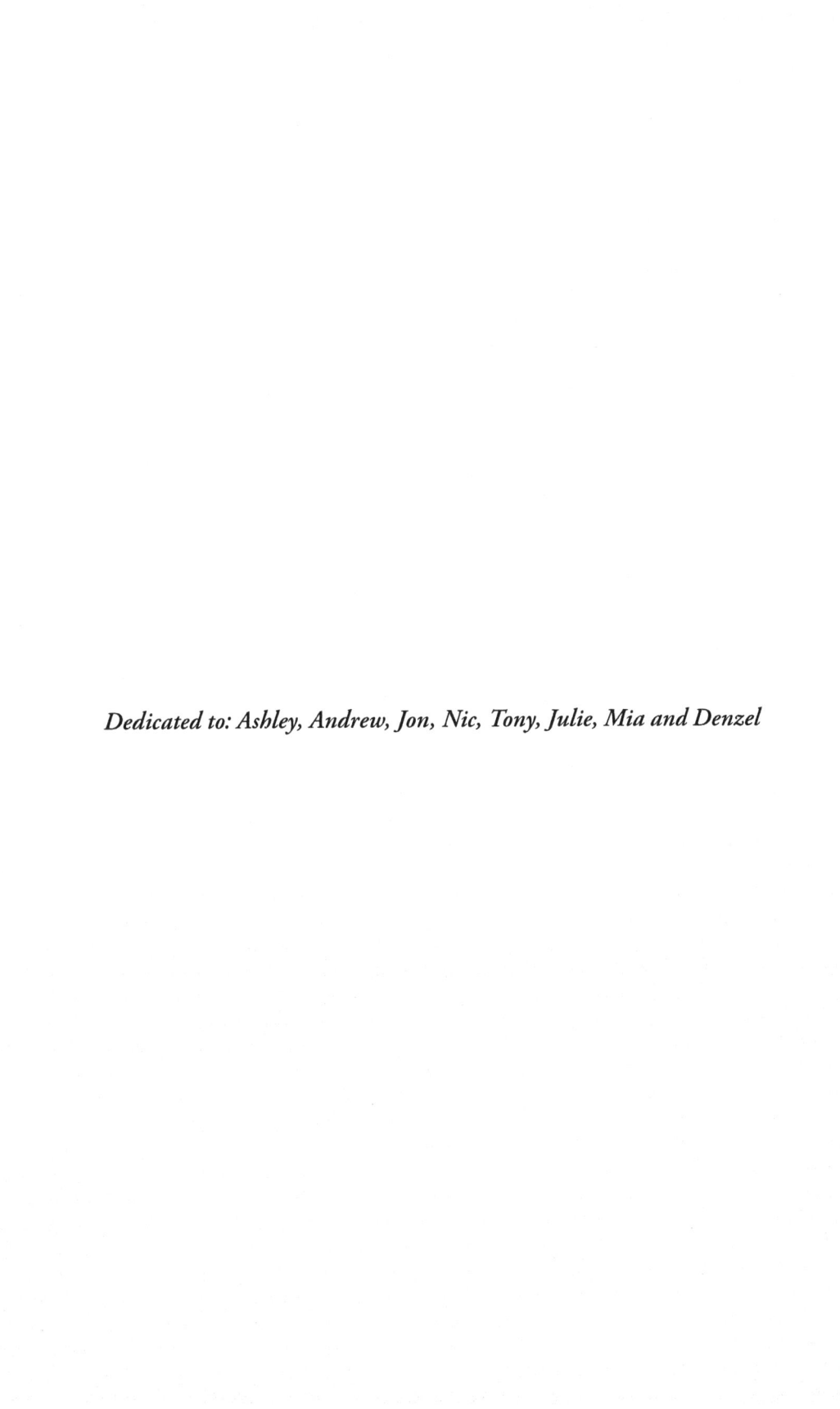

Dedicated to: Ashley, Andrew, Jon, Nic, Tony, Julie, Mia and Denzel

Prelude

It was the summer of 1974 when Kara introduced herself to Sherry. Kara joined their 3rd grade class as the new girl, only a week before school was to let out. Her first day was about a week after Sherry had been jumped at school. One boy had been bullying her all year, but that day he got her on the playground alone and quickly surrounded her with all of his friends.

It was picture day and Sherry was dressed in a beautiful pink dress and white lace socks with shiny new black shoes. Her mother had plaited her hair that morning, and her father had even told her she looked pretty, something that didn't happen very often. But despite all of this, she felt apprehensive about going to school. She didn't know why, but just had a feeling something bad would happen.

As she was thrown to the ground, she lost some skin on her knees. She couldn't see outside the circle of boys and she knew that meant no one could see in either. The boys took turns kicking and shoving her. At one point she tried to get to her feet and she was pushed back and forth around the circle, losing her balance and falling again. She heard them calling her the n-word and telling her she was stupid. Sherry couldn't escape.

For weeks no one would speak to her about it. It was like the attack never happened. She had never felt so alone, and would for many years.

Sherry stood again and managed to break out of the circle, landing again on the ground. Through her tears she searched the playground for a teacher or any adult. She didn't think about being labeled a snitch; she knew what was happening was wrong. She ran towards a Mrs. Talbot, a substitute teacher, and fell into her arms. She sobbed uncontrollably, but felt safe. Mrs. Talbot took her inside and cleaned her up, returning her to her classroom to have some alone time before the other kids came in.

Her teacher, Mrs. Hartliss approached her desk, seeing Sherry crying with her head down and knowing what happened. She leaned in close and whispered softly, "You'll live," before walking away with a smirk on her face.

Several days and a conference with the principal later, the boys had been held responsible, or as responsible as a group of black and white kids beating a black girl in school would be held in those days. But the class and many in the entire school would not forget what happened. It seemed to Sherry that people avoided her even more after the attack. She brushed it off, going back into her shell and looking forward to summer.

Kara was just what Sherry needed, another outsider. Being from California, she was different, and Sherry liked that. The two hit it off right away despite their dramatic differences and forged a friendship that would seem impenetrable.

Chapter One
Powerlines

Sherry was awakened by the chill in her body. It was winter, but the chill wasn't from the air; it had more to do with the feeling in the pit of her stomach. She slid out of bed and onto her knees to pray. *Lord please let it be a calm, quiet morning...unlike the night last night.* The second part snuck into her prayer before she had a chance to stop it. *And thank you for bringing my Dad home last night...even though he was wasted-drunk.* Sherry thought a quick "amen" and stood. She was having a hard time keeping her prayer positive that morning and thought she better stop before she told God something she might regret.

Sherry had heard her father's truck barreling up to the house; it had to have been around 2 a.m. With her bedroom window open, she heard the door of his truck open and him stumble out, humming loudly some song Sherry didn't recognize. *Well, at least he's happy,* she had thought. She never knew how her father would be feeling when he came home drunk. Usually, if the rest of the family was in bed, she didn't have to worry about him losing his temper, though he had woke them all late one night last summer to clean the house, something he had said, should have been done by their "little black asses" long before he got home. That night she prayed the whole time she was cleaning, *Lord, let me get out of this house one day.*

She was referring to the five-room house she shared with her family. Five rooms shared by seven people. Sherry Sweetstone was 10 years old and getting ready for the fifth grade. She was the only girl in the family, aside from her mother Sadie. Larence was the baby. Well, he wasn't *a* baby, but he was the youngest at age 8. Maurice was the next one older than Sherry at 12. She was pretty close to Maurice as he was her protector, the older one who was most often around. Edward was 14 and Mack was 15. Those two stuck together like glue and while they were both the typical protective brothers, they were teenagers and so off doing their own things most of the time. And then, of course, there was her father Red Sweetstone, a mill worker and drinker, but still a man of good character and a relatively good father, and her mother Sadie.

Sherry was a slim and athletic girl. She had long, dark brown hair which she wore loosely pulled back in a ponytail or in two braids. Her skin always looked bronzed, kissed by the sun. She had a pretty round face and brown almond-shaped eyes. Sherry always had an innocent look on her face, definitely not naïve, but maybe a little angelic. But if you knew her well enough, you knew she held some sadness behind those eyes.

It was her daily routine, to say her prayers first thing in the morning, whether it was a school day or if she had slept in on a summer morning. She had done it since her mother showed her when she was very young. The habit just stuck. Some days were better than others, and she would spend several minutes thanking God for her blessings. Then there were days like today, where she couldn't really focus and instead could only think of things that were *wrong*. Sherry pulled on her school clothes and made her way to the bathroom before her brothers woke.

She was grateful to finally have a usable bathroom in the house. She had spent the first eight years of her life rushing outside into the woods to use the outhouse in all types of weather. Sherry's father was gracious enough to build a two-seater inside the rickety shed after years of his children screaming at each other to hurry up. But for years he wasn't willing to put a bathroom in the house. It wasn't like they were living in the dark ages; it was the 1970s and everyone else Sherry knew had a real bathroom. Sherry remembered the days checking for Wolf spiders before sitting on the rough wooden seat. Trying to stay completely still while going number two could be tricky and uncomfortable, but she was convinced if she remained motionless they wouldn't jump on her if they were around. They were more afraid of her than Sherry realized.

Sherry was terrified every time she had to walk down through the woods to the shitter, as the Sweetstones referred to the outhouse. When she was lucky, she could convince one of her brothers to go with her. They would take turns holding the flashlight, a narrow ray of yellow light bouncing off the trees as they stepped. While the company provided a bit of comfort, the fear would move in as she stood outside waiting for her brother to finish his business. Between the outhouse and pumping well water, because there was no running water in the home, it sometimes felt like Sherry was living in the dark ages.

When it was cold, Sherry's father kept a piss bucket in the house so the kids could go number one. But if it was more than peeing that you had to do, you were heading through the woods no matter the weather conditions. Mr. Sweetstone was also generous enough to keep the bucket in Sherry's room, though she was never sure why. So for the first eight years of her life, Sherry had the pleasure of smelling pee while she slept. One day while Sherry's dad carried the full bucket outside to empty it, it bumped against his leg and urine went all over his pants and shoes. It wasn't the two black snakes found inside the back of the outhouse that motivated Red to install a real bathroom. No, it was only being covered in piss that gave him the push to install a toilet and hook up the well water.

It was a school day and Sherry knew her time in the bathroom would be limited. Soon, her brothers would all be clamoring to get in there and use the toilet. So she moved quickly, washing her face and brushing her teeth. Staring in the mirror before she was finished, she poked her chest out a little, wondering if she was finally going to get boobs this summer. A knock on the door startled her back to reality, and she rushed spit the toothpaste from her mouth and rinsed her toothbrush. As she was wiping her face on her towel, Larence came rushing in, holding himself.

"Okay, okay! I'm done." Larence didn't respond and simply slammed the door behind her as she left.

The Sweetstone house was surrounded on all sides by thick woods.

From afar, the smoke coming out of the chimney was the only evidence of the little red brick house. The wooded area was over-populated with snakes and spiders. Back then, the county trucks would ride through the streets spraying a dense fog of pesticides to kill off mosquitos. There were paths that the Boy Scouts made in the woods behind Sherry's house. If you got on them, you could hike for 30 miles. Playing outdoors was the main source of entertainment for the Sweetstone children and all of the kids from nearby River Sades, the big neighborhood across the road. From a young age, they hunted, hiked, went creek-jumping and built tree forts. It was a parent's paradise-- kids didn't sit in the house all day on computers or glued to the television and video games. They went outside after breakfast and would stay out until they were called in at dinner time, usually begging to stay out for another 30 minutes.

Living in the woods was a daily adventure. Both real and imagined creatures could be lurking behind every tree. While you could lose yourself in the fun of it all, it was crucial that you knew the local wildlife. All of the local kids knew the difference between the poisonous and harmless local snakes. They knew what poison ivy looked like and knew how to remove a tick. They weren't "street-wise," but were "wildlife-wise." They had to be or they couldn't be out in the woods all day.

Sherry had her breakfast, some toasted oats and a banana. Her parents didn't waste money on expensive sugary cereals or donuts. They got the basics every day. Sometimes, when her mother had a day off she would cook eggs and bacon for the kids. But usually that was a meal saved for Red Sweetstone. After she ate, Sherry went out on the porch and stared into the distance. She reflected on the dream she had that night. She had forgotten about it with her father's 2 a.m. arrival, but it was a bad one to be sure. She only hoped this was a run-of-the-mill dream and *not* one that would be coming true.

Sherry had been having prophetic dreams for years. She first realized it when she was about six, helping her mother with her cleaning business and *knowing* the homes before she entered them. But she was just a baby then and didn't realize the importance of what was happening. She could still remember the day it actually hit her that she was dreaming the future and the impact those dreams could have…

Maurice was in charge of all the kids on summer days when their parents were both working. He wasn't the oldest but this freed up the other two to go out and do their own thing on summer days. He was inside watching television, no doubt, while Sherry was outside playing. It was the summer before third grade and Sherry was eight-years old. Sherry saw Pete Barnes walking up the driveway. Pete was an attractive boy and got a lot of attention from the girls of River Sades. He was a good kid, for the most part, and had come to ask if he and some other kids could use the short cut on the Sweetstone property to get to the powerlines.

The powerlines was the spot where your parents couldn't find you, and where you moved up in the ranks among the other River Sades kids. You won a certain level of respect for even knowing how to get there, and for the fact that you had the courage to jump the wide mouth of the creek. The trek there was not an easy stretch of terrain. When the path ended, you had to hike three miles under and over brush, brier and sticker bushes. The mouth of the creek was a culmination of the treachery up until that point. This body of water ran parallel to the Severn River that dumped into the Chesapeake Bay. You needed a running start to make it to the other side. The key was knowing the perfect spot to jump over. There was only one spot on the other side of the creek that was safe for landing. Anyone who made this hike to the powerlines had to be a good athlete and good at keeping quiet; they weren't to give directions to anyone.

"Yeah, sure," said Maurice, silently wishing he could tag along. This was a young kid's dream. Pete was older than Maurice, very athletic and a bit of a show-off, something younger kids were drawn to. Maurice himself was a bit of a show-off and a budding athlete. Pete was his neighborhood idol. Maurice never got much positive feedback or "attaboy"s from their father, but the older kids in River Sades always picked him for their teams when they divided up for sports. For him, that was confirmation enough. Unfortunately, Maurice would seek that validation from outsiders for many years to come.

Pete was well-mannered with pretty blue eyes, a strong chiseled face with the body to match and dirty blonde hair. Captain of his high school football team, Pete was raised to give proper respect to parents, always saying "yes ma'am" and "no sir." It's because of this that Mr. Sweetstone liked all of the Barnes children; they were welcome on his property anytime.

Taking initiative to invite himself, confident that Pete wouldn't mind, Maurice turned to Sherry pointing his finger in her face and swearing her to secrecy. "I'll take you with me Sherry," like he had a choice. "You can come if you promise not to tell on me for taking you or tell where it is." She nodded her response.

The two packed up water and snacks. Sherry felt special. The older kids talked about things she couldn't understand. But despite her young age, they were very kind to her. Being around them, she laughed a lot, partially because they were funny, but also because she was a little nervous. "So this is what older kids get to do," she thought, giddy with excitement.

All of the Sweetstone kids ended up coming along that day. It was rare for all five to be together by choice, especially as Edward and Mack got older and made friends outside of the normal circle of River Sades' kids.

The summer breeze was light and the afternoon sun was shining bright and hot. Sherry looked up at the sky, which she did a lot. It was beautiful—perfectly blue without a cloud in sight. The smell of summer was in the air, and even for a young child, this smell had meaning. It was the clean smell of sweat after running through field, blossoms on the trees, and the smoke off of her father's grill—it was nostalgia. She could hear in the distance the lumber mill. It warmed her heart having her father work so close to home; she felt safe in the woods with him only being a mile away.

The hike was about five miles. Then the path ended and they reached the mouth of the creek. All joking stopped and conversations faded to whispers. Sherry knew it was a serious time. Her brother's friends drew straws, gambling on who would jump first to the other side. Whoever was the first to go would chart the exact route for the others. Pete, who was really macho, drew the shortest straw, meaning he would jump first. Everyone looked to Sherry. The teenagers knew she was too small to stretch her legs for a jump like that.

Pete looked too and said, "Hop on." He squatted down to the ground to give Sherry a piggy back ride. There was a little apprehension in her movements, but she was on his back before her worries got the best of her. She saw the large mouth of the creek and knew water moccasins often laid in wait along the bank. She also knew that they were at a deep part of the creek and Sherry couldn't swim.

Sherry whispered in Pete's ear, "I can't swim."

"It's okay. I can." he said with such assurance that Sherry believed his ability to swim would somehow save her. She thought Pete was cute and would have believed anything he said.

Pete jumped with ease like a star football player, leaving Sherry to wonder, "Am I that light or is Pete really that strong?"

Everyone else made the jump including Maurice who was just beginning to understand that coming out hiking and bringing Sherry was not his best idea. Maurice wasn't a swimmer either and wasn't entirely comfortable with looking out for his own ass at the power lines, let alone Sherry's. He was beginning to question his decision to let her tag along.

Walking over a short, thickly overgrown hill, Sherry reached to move the brush out of her face and looked through. The clearing on the other side was breathtaking. She felt as if she had been here before. She stood still for a moment. *I know I haven't been here before but it looks, feels, even smells familiar.* Taking it all in, she remembered why it seemed familiar. She had dreamt about this place. In her dream, this place was magical. Amazed, Sherry stood in a daze for about ten minutes trying to rationalize how she could possibly have dreamt about the exact place without ever having been here before. The hills, the blowing grass, even the people with her were exactly as she had seen them in her sleep. The feeling wasn't completely unique to her.

She had first started recognizing the dreams when she was about six. When she would wake up she would remember being in a house she never had never been in before. And like she was experiencing now at the power lines, she could still sense the home when she woke up, right down to the smell.

Sherry's mom was a housekeeper. She would often take Sherry to help her clean homes. Sherry would have the task of dumping trash and ash trays. It was pretty humiliating because her mother worked for some of Sherry's friends in River Sades. But, it didn't take long for Sherry to get over it. Her friends and their parents were nice people and didn't seem to care or judge her for it. For years Sherry dreamt of different houses. When Sherry was exposed to the houses on her mother's schedule she realized she was in familiar surroundings. She would walk in a new home and realize she had seen the entire interior and exterior before, but said nothing to anyone.

One particular house she could see in her sleep had a red and black checkered ash tray. One fall day Sherry's mother took her to work on her first job. Her mother made it very clear before they got out of the truck that she was to walk through the house and gather only the trash and ash trays, being careful not to disturb the things, or any people that might be in the home.

The house was dark and dank. It smelled like moth balls. No surprise then that two old people lived here. It was cramped and filled to the brim with old furniture. Sherry made her way through, noticing the candy in old-people candy dishes scattered all over the tables. She glanced over her shoulders, thinking she could grab a peppermint patty. A cough startled her; there was Mr. Cane, six-foot-one with receding gray hair, gasping for air. He was sprawled on the couch, feet hanging off the edge, wearing a black and red lumberjack shirt. The table in front of him was filled with ash trays and he had a cigarette hanging from his mouth.

Between the coughs and gasps, he managed a "Hello little lady— help yourself!" From the coughs that followed, it seemed that little bit of conversation almost killed him.

Sherry managed a quiet "Hi." and stepped next to Mr. Cane, reaching across him to the table. She grabbed one of the ash trays that looked as if it were about to spill over. She carefully lifted the precarious container to the garbage bag she was carrying. The moment she turned it over, she immediately recognized the red and black checkered tray from her dream. She stood frozen, confused and wondering how she could have known this ashtray would be here, how she could have experienced this very same motion before while she was asleep in her bed. She hoped her frozen body language didn't make Mr. Cane think she was uncomfortable in his home—though she kind of was-- watching him roll around on his couch trying to catch his breath, exposing her to his deep, deathly coughs. Sherry was not easily frightened, especially of old people, but Mr. Cane's size and the volume of his coughing was a bit unnerving.

At age six it was obvious to Sherry that the universe was speaking to

Iceburg

her through her dreams. And it was obvious that Mr. Cane needed to quit smoking.

Sherry wasn't sure what it meant but she knew it was magical.

Back at the power lines, though, something felt different. Sherry remembered in her dream that something scary happened. She felt it in her stomach, a feeling of anticipation. She tried to remember the dream, but like dreams sometimes do, the exact scenes escaped her. She tried to push the thoughts out of her head and enjoy this new experience.

There were rolling green hills for miles and one telephone pole after another in perfect sequence, wires stretching from one to the next like heavy jump ropes waiting to be turned. The grass was bright green, looking fresh and spring-like, and you could see motorbike trails pressing the grass flat and curving in wild, roving patterns. Sherry knew the place had been a tradition among River Sades kids for years, perhaps generations. Now, with her, it was being passed down again. There was not a speck of trash on the ground in sight, surprising since there were no garbage cans and the place was only frequented by kids.

The older kids pulled out cigarettes and began to smoke. Sherry watched as her brother went off somewhere. Sherry wasn't sure if her brother was smoking. Neither did she care. This was huge to be at the power lines with teenagers and she would not turn into a snitch. Across on the north side of the valley, Sherry saw in the distance what she thought was a man leaning on a fence with a dog. She squinted her eyes and thought she could see a gun. *Oh my God,* she thought. The memory came back to her. She could remember this man from her dream, and in that dream she remembered hearing a gun shot. Sherry was scared motionless as she watched Pete, the leader of the pack, heading north with some other kids where you could see a huge mansion and farm house in the distance. She watched as they walked across the valley and began climbing the hill on the other side, wondering how far they had walked as they shrank in the distance and wondering if they saw the man they were approaching too.

She thought of screaming, of calling out. But, how would she explain herself? And who would believe her? She didn't know what to do and didn't want to risk being wrong. If that was who she thought it was, he was full of piss and vinegar, as her mother would say, but wouldn't actually *do* anything.

Maurice and Josie were at the back of the pack, taking their time and just getting ready to start the climb up the hill. Looking up they saw Ol' Man Taylor waiting for them. Six-two and dressed in his farmer brown clothes, holding a long-barreled gun in his right hand, he was quite a ways off but the boys would know him anywhere. They both screamed frantically while waving their hands signaling for Pete and the rest of the group to turn around. Already climbing the hill, the other boys couldn't see the man holding the rifle. Pete was looking down at his feet. He thought it made the climb quick and easy if he didn't continue to look up to see how far he had to go. He stopped and looked back. Then he threw his hand up hoping to hold the others back. "Wait," said Pete "are they calling us?"

He saw that Maurice was pointing for him to look up. When he did, all Pete could see was bushes and grass. He stepped to the side of the shrubbery blocking his view and saw they were twenty yards from a loaded hunting rifle. Ol' Man Taylor shot up in the air one time and yelled, "You kids get the hell out of here! You see this sign--no trespassing!"

Pete and the gang took off running in the other direction, back down the hill and towards Sherry and the other kids. They were leaping in strides to get back down the hill before Taylor fired another round. Beating the others back to where Sherry was, Maurice grabbed her by her shirt and pulled her with him. They took off running, jumping back over the creek with Josie following. Pete and the others ran across the meadow-valley, through the trees and over the creek. By the time they stopped running they were laughing hysterically. "Did you see the look on Taylor's face?"

"Get off my property!" The teenagers took turns saying it over and over in their best old-man voice. The more they said it, the more they laughed. Sherry felt a little out of the loop. She didn't understand what was so funny-- she was still scared. She would understand years later, but eight years old was a little young to find humor in being shot at. It was an adrenalin rush for the older kids. At her young age, adrenalin was equated with fear and nothing else.

Sherry's older brother waved his hand signaling that it was time to head back. It was nearing dusk and it would be pitch black before they got home if they didn't hurry. They needed *some* light to spot the path from the power lines; it was hard enough to make out in the daylight. Being one of the oldest there, Edward knew if anything happened to his younger siblings he would be to blame. Sherry knew he was a good brother, a caretaker. He turned everyone around for their wellbeing.

On the way back the boys were coasting slowly on their motorbikes as Sherry and her other siblings were alongside, kicking up the leaves at a slow jog. Suddenly, Edward shouted "Snake!" and the children took off as if they were Olympic runners, leaving Sherry and her younger brother Larence behind. Sherry's shoes were untied and as she started to run she fell down, skinning her knee. As she picked her face off of the ground, she could hear the creek and looked to the right to see a little of the water glistening through the trees. As she turned and looked over to her left, there was a huge five-foot water moccasin curled up, lying in the hillside to left of the path where she had fallen.

She screamed "Edward!" Edward quickly turned his motorbike. He sped over to Sherry, and in what seemed like one swift move, scooped her up and put her on the back of his bike, driving off like a bat out of hell. Remembering Larence, Sherry's other older brother Mack swooped him up in the same way. Their father would be proud of the boys if he saw how they reacted with such animal instinct, protecting the young. As Sherry rode, holding on tight to Edward's waist, she realized the path must have become a mating ground for the black snakes--they were everywhere. She wondered how they had missed them on their way out to the power lines. She wondered how close they had come to being bit.

The path was muddy and there was one last hill to climb, then down again into the Sweetstone property. Being a tomboy, and not having much of a choice with four brothers, Sherry knew how to be a passenger on the back of her brothers Vespa. They flew around one curve to the next, passing a few of the other kids who were on foot. As they approached the hill, Sherry prayed to God they would make it up. It was muddy and the mud made for a slippery and treacherous climb on the bike. Edward was a skilled rider, but when they got to the foot of the hill the bike stalled out. Edward quickly restarted the bike but the mud was so thick they couldn't get traction and kept sliding around. Edward tried taking off slow, but the tires would just spin. The kids on foot quickly caught up; as a matter of fact it surprised Sherry how fast they got to the foot of the hill. They were running, and as they ran by Sherry heard them hollering "Snake!"

The sounds of running and the echoes of their voices pierced the now-darkness. Edward and Sherry knew they had to get the heck out of there. Edward turned around and started heading back into the direction of the snakes Sherry buried her head into his back, not entirely sure what it was he was planning, but trusting in her older brother nonetheless. Suddenly Edward wheeled his bike around in the direction of the hill towards home. He screamed, "Hang on tight Sherry!" He gave it all the gas the Vespa would provide. They went flying through the mud as if they were in one of those motocross races, and up the hill. As the bike hit the top of the hill, Sherry felt her stomach in her throat as it felt like they were suspended in midair. The Vespa dropped and flew down the other side and onto their property.

It took Sherry more than a minute to realize they were okay and they were out of danger. After her heart rate had normalized, she kept seeing herself and Edward fly over the hill like in some kind of action movie. She always knew Edward would do anything for her, but that moment elevated him to hero status in her little-girl mind.

Sherry went back inside from the porch and climbed the stairs to check on Larence. It seemed like it was always the duty of the kid one age up to check on their closest younger sibling. Sherry knew he was awake after their bathroom encounter, but Larence wasn't necessarily a morning person and she wouldn't put it past him to crawl back in the bed. She saw through his cracked door that he was up and getting ready for school. Both her and Larence's bedroom doors were made of thin wood panels. It was some cheap creation that afforded very little privacy, something that she had grown accustomed to in this house.

Sherry was excited—today was the fourth day and she could get back on the school bus. She was suspended from the bus for three days for fighting, well really for kicking two peoples' butts. It wasn't a fair fight and she knew it.

Chapter 2
Always-Fighting

Sherry peered at Larence through his door, rubbing his eyes and looking so innocent, thinking about how special her little brother was to her. She felt she needed to protect him ever since he got bit by Lieutenant, the dog that lived on Perch Run Road. Sherry had dreamed prior to the incident weeks before it happened. She could see Lieutenant standing on his hind legs with his mouth around Larence's head. Larence had gone to retrieve a ball that had rolled into Lieutenant's territory. The massive German Shepard was viscous and always fastened to a chain when visitors were around to play with the children who owned him. Sherry had to convince herself that the dog was just playing with Larence in her dream, hoping that by believing the dog was just being playful, no attack would happen. Sherry stayed away from Lieutenant even when he was on the chain. If he saw you around, he would take off running like a bat out of hell, only stopping when his chain ran out. But each time, he would run like he was going to break the chain, and Sherry believed he could do it.

It was just last summer when Larence went to retrieve the ball that had landed near the dog, thinking nothing of Lieutenant--after all, everyone was outside playing. At the very edge of Lieutenant's boundary, Larence snuck to pick up the ball. He thought he could get away safely and knew the key was to not make any noise to draw Lieutenant's attention to him. He crouched low, tiptoeing through the grass and finally reaching his little fingers out to grab the ball. But Lieutenant spotted him and by the time Larence realized it, it was too late.

He jumped on Larence's back as Larence turned to run, standing on his hind legs to hold him. Larence froze and screamed to the other children. He was panicking, but had enough sense to realize he had better do something quick before Lieutenant began feasting on him. So he helped himself by lunging forward out of Lieutenant's paws. As he moved forward, the chain stopped the dog but he managed to latch on to the flesh of Larence's ear, tearing it. It wasn't a huge injury, but enough to leave a small scar and to terrify Sherry. She immediately flashed to her dream, seeing Lieutenant on his hind legs with his mouth around Laurence's head. She knew at that moment she would need to pay more attention to these dreams, particularly if they involved members of her family. She began to grasp the seriousness of her prophetic dreams as each new one came to fruition.

Waiting for her brother to be ready for school, Sherry thought, *I'm glad this year's almost over.* It had been a tough school year, particularly since it was just her and Larence on the elementary bus with all the Desy Cove kids. The kids of Desy Cove were notorious for being racist and ignorant. Up until last year, Maurice was on the bus too, so she never felt completely at risk. Sherry remembered the years where all three of them would get on the bus together, having to listen to the other kids calling them the n-word and fighting white children all the way to school. Thankfully last year, near the end of the school year, a high schooler missed his bus and caught the middle school bus instead. He was already on when the Sweetstones were picked up from their stop that morning and Sherry recognized him as knowing Edward.

That particular morning, Sherry and Maurice had decided they were going to fight like their life depended on it if harassed by the other kids. They were tired of being called names and taunted for everything and anything. Sherry and her brothers could fight and their father always told them, that name calling was one thing, but never let them put their hands on you. Sherry thought her father's advice on this point was just a little hypocritical, considering he dished enough of that around to last a life time.

When it came to the kids on the bus, Maurice would always jump up and stand in front of the seat where the three sat to protect his younger siblings. William McDonald was usually leading the taunts, threatening the Sweetstone kids and laying into Maurice with the worst names he could come up with. But this time would be different. When the rednecks, as Sherry's father described them, came towards the back of the bus with plans to start things up as usual, Sherry and Maurice were ready. William was there, as usual, and started in, calling Maurice a greasy n-.

"Say it to my face," Maurice said back, looking cool as ice.

William took about five steps closer and Maurice stood to meet him. Sherry knew Maurice wasn't scared of William. If all of his friends jumped in, it would be a different story. Sherry stood up from her seat and so did Larence, a strong united front ready to kick some redneck ass.

David Dale, the high schooler, was sitting about two rows in front of the Sweetstones. He wasn't prejudice and was mature enough not to believe the lies of his father about race. He was refreshing, a good kid and tried to lead the Desy Cove kids, showing them that they should not follow the crowd and hate someone for the color of their skin. Some of the kids on the bus that morning were in Sherry's class. They would say hi in school but never on the bus. Sherry hated them for that and knew she couldn't trust them.

As William came closer he broke into a quick stride coming towards Maurice with his right hand balled into a fist. Out of nowhere David caught his fist. Towering about a foot over William he spoke through his teeth, "William, sit your dumb ass down." William walked backwards a few steps, turning red as he turned around and headed back to his seat.

"What's up Maurice," said David, sitting back down and looking out of the window like nothing had happened.

Maurice, Sherry, and Larence sat down slowly. Maurice looked surprised and relieved. He had never really spoken to David and had no idea why he would stick up for a younger black kid. But Sherry and her brothers were grateful, not really worrying too much about David's motivation. He was one of the cool kids for sure, thought Edward, the kind that did what he wanted no matter what other kids thought.

David sat staring out the window thinking of what those kids might have had to go through when there was no one here to stick up for them. The older boy had some balls, he thought, to be able to stand up for himself like that.

"William!" David shouted over the heads of other bus riders. William turned but didn't say anything. "Leave my friend Maurice alone man, or you are going to have much bigger problems."

Sherry and Maurice looked at one another and smiled. Too bad David hadn't missed his bus earlier in the year.

"Yeah William, why you gotta be such a jerk?" said a Desy Cove kid that was sitting near the front of the bus. Whispers and snide comments directed at William traveled the length of the bus, and for the final few weeks of the school year, there were no problems for the Sweetstones on this bus either.

Fighting for Dignity

Edward and Mack Sweetstone were inseparable; they were the oldest of the Sweetstone clan. Despite being the younger of the two, Edward always seemed to be the leader. Both paved the way for their other siblings' survival, being surrounded by two all-white communities-- Desy Cove, where it was clear that blacks weren't welcome, and River Sades where no blacks lived. But the Sweetstones, living just outside of River Sades, were the exception. It seemed they didn't fit the naïve and limited description of what River Sades' residents thought black people were. Though there weren't any blacks in River Sades, the residents there were embarrassed of their neighbors in Desy Cove, and largely thought of them as white trash. While River Sades folks were sheltered and had limited experiences with minorities, they thought themselves to be above the ignorance down the road.

Edward was an honest teenager who loved hard work. He had a beautiful smile showing his white teeth against his deep chocolate skin. He was strong and often helped his father with cutting and selling wood on the weekends to make extra money. Mack had honey skin and shared his brother's ability to light up a room with his smile. Both boys were Boy

Scouts and both were very handsome--Mack was tall and lanky while Edward had more of a football player build.

While they weren't the only blacks at their rundown high school, there were few others and they were definitely the only ones on this bus route. Because of where the Sweetstones lived, they were stuck on the bus with all of the Desy Cove kids. Needless to say, their bus ride to school was a living hell. But the Sweetstone boys definitely had thick skin and it grew thicker as they learned to ignore the ignorant taunting and being called out their name by the kids in Desy Cove. Their only saving grace was a handful of good friends they met in Boy Scouts and the other kids from Perch Run Road, where the Sweetstones lived, that allowed them to tolerate the daily bus ride.

Mack and Edward knew better than to go into Desy Cove alone. But the community had the only candy store for miles. When they did travel they took their bicycles, and you could guarantee they would be chased out with the n-word following. The worst of the bunch was the hillbillies of Desy Cove--not that there was much class difference to separate one Desy Cove resident from the next. The Kulley family stood out with their rumored-incestuous behavior. Nate, Buck, Troy, Will, Brenda and Jenny terrorized their neighborhood and gave Mack and Edward hell.

One night Red Sweetstone, who was a towering six-foot-four with a strong chiseled face and almond skin reminiscent of his Cherokee ancestors, had awakened everyone by shouting through the house, "Jesus Christ!"

Red shuffled around, putting clothes on while calling for Edward and Mack to get up. Mr. Sweetstone was very light sleeper. He knew some folks would rather he take his family somewhere else, where there were other "coloreds." But he knew where he was and was not leaving regardless of the threating phone calls, intimidating stares, or even the blowing up of his mail box. He had five children and wanted them to have better than he had growing up. So in 1960 he moved out of the city and into the country for a better job and a safe place to raise a family. He reached high on his cabinet feeling around in the dark for his box of bullets. Grabbing a handful, he ran to the door practically tearing it off the hinges. As he rushed by the mantle, he grabbed his twelve-gauge shotgun. Mack and Edward kneeled on their beds peering out their window, their shadows cascading throughout the bedroom. They found themselves staring at a cross engulfed in flames directly in front of their home.

Mr. Sweetstone yelled for his sons again, his boys were the only back-up he had for miles. They both jumped up and ran to the call of their father. Mr. Sweetstone grabbed his other gun, a twenty-two and threw it to Edward. The three went out the back door. Mr. Sweetstone yelled to Mack to get water from the well. It was an old hand-pump well that stood around the side of their house. Mack pumped as fast as he could to get to fill the buckets with water and ran over to throw them one-by-one on the fire. The boys repeated it this until the flame was out.

Mr. Sweetstone had loaded both guns and fired two rounds into the air. Then he listened for movement. Suddenly in the darkness of the woods, he heard leaves rustling. Someone was running. He hollered at the boys to bring him a flashlight. While he didn't want to make a bad situation any worse, he would have loved to get his hands on whoever found humor in terrorizing his family. Mr. Sweetstone was afraid of no man, and he didn't play around when it came to his family. The three searched in the surrounding woods for what felt like hours, but the punks from Desy Cove got away. On the walk back to the house, Edward and Mack informed their father of the daily hardship they were enduring on the bus ride to school, though they didn't say they suspected the Kulleys of the cross-burning, Red was a smart man. Their father had realized they would experience bullying, but he hadn't really grasped the fear they were experiencing as a result until he walked with them that night in the woods. After seeing their own home attacked, the dynamic changed. The thought of his children fearing for their own safety would keep him up many nights, patrolling his yard after the slightest sound.

He stopped in the grass outside the back door and turned to Edward and Mack. "If I'm not here and anyone, I mean *anyone*, steps on this property threatening you, your mother, or anyone else in this family, you have my permission to run' em off at gun point." He looked them deep in the eyes, first one and then the other. "You boys understand?"

"Yes sir," the boys said in unison, both empowered and scared at what their father had just given them permission to do.

The police were called out that night and took a report. A few days later someone called Sherry's house to speak to her father. The person on the other end of the phone was a member of the Black Panthers Party, from an all-black neighborhood eight miles away. Sherry was shocked to know that there were all-black neighborhoods anywhere near her. The few black children she saw in school weren't in her grade and she didn't know where they lived. But, when she passed them in the hallways, she was glad to see them. Red declined the offer for help, though he was thankful for the phone call. He had kids to raise and worked hard to raise them without instilling anything even remotely resembling hate or superiority. He always said, "You are no better than anyone and no one is better than you, regardless of the color of skin." That and, "Be proud to be who God made you," were a few of his favorite adages.

Several weeks went by and the Kulleys thought they were untouchable. Often the kids from River Sades would visit Edward and Mack; they would play kickball or basketball in the Sweetstone yard. This Saturday in particular Edward and Mack had no friends come over because they had were forced to spend the day raking leaves, no easy feat considering the amount of trees between the house and the road. The two had just come out of the shed holding two rakes and wearing their work gloves and were walking towards the ditch near the driveway. They decided to start with the hardest part of the yard first, so everything else would go easily. As they were heading in that direction, they saw a group of kids in the distance coming over the hill out of Desy Cove. It took a few minutes of straining, but the boys knew from the shapes of the oncoming bodies and their we-mean-business swagger that it was the Kulleys.

"What do they want?" said Mack, innocently curious and without a bit of fear in his voice. "It's a little odd for them to be out of their neighborhood during the daytime."

The Kulleys knew better than to come towards River Sades, particularly if they were alone; they were hated there. All four Kulley boys were headed straight in Mack and Edward's direction. Nate was out front with Troy and Will kicking cans and whistling behind. Buck, the meanest of the gang, had a belt in his hand and was slapping it onto his other hand. In something out of a horror movie, the always-disheveled boys broke out into a chant saying, "Kill! Kill! Kill!" and began throwing rocks at Mack and Edward. The Sweetstone boys dropped their rakes and ran inside to get their father. Red got up from his chair, where he had sat with a drink and the newspaper, and looked out the window. He could hear the boys calling his sons outside and using the N word to do it. Red looked at his sons and said, "Go shut 'em up."

Mack's eyes widened. He didn't want to seem like a coward to his father, but they were clearly outnumbered. He said quietly, "But, there are four of them."

"You want a bully to leave you alone?" Red said calmly. "You can't depend on your daddy to take care of it." His voice rose considerably, "You gotta stand up to him!"

Edward and Mack were more afraid of their father than the Kulleys, and they would rather get beat by the boys outside than that man in the house.

As if reading their mind, their father said, "If you don't go outside and whip their ass, I'm whippin' yours."

That was all the motivation they needed. Edward and Mack flew out the door, down the driveway and onto the street. Though it scared them, their father's motivational speech lit a fire under the boys and got them a little riled up.

"It's on," Edward said seriously, giving Mack a look that Mack had really never seen in his younger brother. "For years this son of a bitch has taunted me for no reason; at least no reason I could control," thought Edward. "I'll take Buck."

Their father had taught them that the bully with the biggest mouth is often the biggest chicken. Though Edward was ready to confront Buck, he was silently hoping his father's words would prove true.

Buck was on them in what seemed like seconds, swinging his belt at Edward. Edward ducked, reaching out his hand and catching the wild end of the belt. He ripped it out of Buck's left hand. Buck must have been shocked that this kid who took his lip for so long had any fight in him. Edward reached out and hit Buck with a left upper cut and cross right, knocking him flat on his ass.

Iceburg

Mack was wrestling in the road with Nate. Nate was losing the match by a long shot, despite the kicks that Mack was getting from the other Kulley boys. It was obvious to the Sweetstone boys that all these years the Kulleys were all bark and no bite. Edward turned to see Mack getting kicked in the sides and dove on top of Will and Troy, making them crash onto the paved road. The two struggled to get up and took off running. Edward watched, glorying in the view of their backs as they left.

"We're just messing around man," Nate gasped, begging for Mack to let him up.

Edward looked at Buck, standing off to the side, seeming torn between running away and helping Nate.

"You guys come back here again, and you won't be leaving," Edward said to the two remaining Kulley boys.

Word spread quickly about the Kulley defeat. The Sweetstone boys no longer had to worry about the taunting, the racial slurs, and the extreme discomfort and even fear as they rode the Desy Cove school bus to the high school. Their father was right. If they hadn't stood up to the Kulleys, the bullying would have never ended. It took the Kulleys attack to spur their dad's permission to fight, but the self-defense was well executed indeed.

Edward and Mack were able to go in and out of Desy Cove with no problem. They cut grass and did odd jobs to make money. The older folks in the community might not have liked their kind, but they weren't as stupid or as classless as the Kulley kids. The boys were able to buy candy from the Desy Cove corner store whenever they wanted without worrying about not making it home.

Sherry's Fight

Sherry's reassurance about the kids on the bus being nice was short lived. The new year had brought new kids to Desy Cove and it seemed like their eyes couldn't get enough of Sherry and Larence. They were always staring. Sherry couldn't wait to ride on the bus with Kara and her friends from River Sades. Because of where the Sweetstones lived, across but not *in* River Sades, they were on the Desy Cove bus route—at least for now. That would soon change when Sherry switched schools next year. But for now, it felt like the back woods white trash kids were trying to make her life miserable. For some reason the ride *to* school was the worst, something about starting the day with these creeps staring her down really pissed her off.

Though she and Larence seemed to get stared at, they didn't really get picked on much in those first weeks. Ben and Jasmine Moon were the new kids on the bus ride and they were the main targets of the bullying. Jasmine got picked on the most. She was a tomboy with a feminine name. There were rumors about her being gay and getting caught in bed with another girl, though Sherry didn't know how true those were. But, for months Jasmine starred Sherry's friend Kara up and down. It was obvious that she was a tomboy. She showed up to Sherry's P.E. class one day while everyone was stretching, wearing a raggedy red shirt, oversized blue shorts, and tube socks (the kind with the stripes at the top) pulled up over her hairy, pale calves. No girl Sherry knew would ever wear something like that. Jasmine was thin, pale and very average looking with a shadow of a mustache and long stringy brown hair. She was about 5 feet six inches and walked like a man like a man. Even girls their age walked with a little bit of a shimmy in their hips; Sherry thought it was uncontrollable until she saw Jasmine.

Unbeknownst to Sherry, her brothers were actually friends with Jasmine's older brothers. The year was 1979 and Sherry had one more year to move to the middle school-high school, one more year until she could join her older brothers and automatically fit in with the older kids, or so she thought. She figured her brothers were popular and so she would have to be too. For now, she attended Centennial Elementary School built in 1976. Because of the over-population in Eastern Maryland's school district, most of the friends Sherry grew up with would be separated when they got to middle and high school.

Sherry could not figure out how she and Jasmine got off on the wrong foot. She believed it all started on the bus ride to school. After staring Sherry down for weeks, Sherry had finally had enough.

"What is your FREAKING problem?" Sherry shouted across the bus aisle.

"You!" Jasmine countered.

Apparently that was all that needed to be said to create the rift that would ultimately push Sherry to her limit.

Iceburg

Sherry and Jasmine were both very athletic. So in gym class, when it came time to divide into teams, one would get picked for one side and the opposing group would choose the other girl. One particular day, Jasmine was playing goalie, wearing one of those orange mesh, pull-on jerseys over her shirt to show her team. Sherry was in her regular gym clothes on the opposite team. Sherry had taken a verbal beating for weeks from Jasmine. Jasmine would stick out her foot when Sherry came walking by or she would push her whenever the teacher wasn't looking. And she was always threatening to kick Sherry's ass. Wherever they were, Jasmine would stare her down like she was burning holes through Sherry's head. When Larence started giving reports to Sherry that he was being harassed by her too, Sherry drew the line. Larence was a strong young guy for his age, but Jasmine needed an even match and he wasn't it. Jasmine was twice Larence's height and weight, and it wasn't like she was some sissy-girl.

Sherry was very talented at sports and dodge ball was a piece of cake for her. Seeing Jasmine in the goalie box brought her great joy-- all she needed was the ball. Sherry made two quick moves to get open and the ball came straight to her. She stretched out to catch it and spun around. Her teammate faked out the defender protecting Jasmine and Sherry had her chance. It was like the dodge ball gods wanted her to clobber this bully. In the split second that she had, Sherry remembered all the comments and stares, all the pushes, trips, and especially the fact that Jasmine Moon had been tormenting her little brother. From a place deep inside her where she apparently stored up all of her anger, she rocketed the ball at top speed, aiming directly at Jasmine's head. When the ball hit her face, the noise was unmistakable. Girls on both teams gasped when it bounced off the high gymnasium ceiling. Jasmine immediately fell to the floor. Sherry's stomach sank, thinking she was in certain trouble. Luckily, Coach J had no clue that the girls hated each other and yelled, "Score!"

Sherry's teammates cautiously cheered, no one really knowing if Jasmine was okay. Jasmine got to her feet, face flushed with embarrassment and eyes filling with tears of frustration as a few girls started to laugh. No one really liked Jasmine; she hadn't made it exactly easy. Sherry's first reaction was to go see if Jasmine was okay, but the anger in her held her back. She needed to make her point, and going to check on Jasmine would make her look like she wasn't committed to her action. "That will teach you to mess with me," thought Sherry, hoping Jasmine would back off after she got over the humiliation.

It only got worse from that day on. The two exchanged horrible words and taunts at every opportunity. Sherry had a lot of friends; they kind of provided a cushion making her untouchable to Jasmine. Because Sherry couldn't be touched, Jasmine did what any low-life, coward-of-a-bully would do—she focused her attention to Larence.

One day Sherry was sick and stayed home from school. She was able to lie around, nap, and think of everything *but* school and Jasmine Moon. She had an unsettled feeling all day, but she assumed it was the bug her body was fighting and shook it off. All the lazing about, however, changed the moment Larence got home. Sherry recognized the sound of the breaks on the school bus and soon heard Larence's voice, hollering for Sherry. Pound-pound-pound, his feet raced up the stairs and he threw open the door. His face was flushed and he was obviously upset.

"What's wrong Larence—are you okay?" Sherry immediately forgot about not feeling well and flew up off the couch to check on her brother's wellbeing. Realizing she forgot to pray for him in her day long lay-about, Sherry's stomach dropped at the sound of fright in his voice. She had felt that Jasmine may take advantage of her absence, and pick on Larence. True to her instincts, Larence told her what she already knew.

Larence sat in the middle of the bus on the ride home with one of his friends from River Sades, believing that the feud was only between Jasmine and Sherry, or at least thinking that Jasmine wouldn't do anything *too* bad to a little kid. Jasmine had noticed that Sherry wasn't on the bus today and was excited she would have a chance to hurt her without really having to physically confront her—she would do it by hurting her little brother. When he went to get off the bus, Jasmine got ready; a combination of nerves and excitement filled her. The thought that Larence was smaller and innocent didn't bother her at all; as a matter of fact, it set her mind at ease a little because she knew he wouldn't be a challenge.

The bus stopped at Larence's driveway. He got up to get off, saying goodbye to his friends. He didn't see Jasmine stick out her foot, exposing her ragged tennis shoe. Larence tripped over Jasmine's giant foot and his

Iceburg

books went flying. He managed to he kept his balance somehow. He was smart enough to immediately look back and see the foot being snatched back. His eyes followed the ragged shoe to the leg that led to the face of Jasmine Moon, smirking and looking a little too proud of herself. Larence felt his face getting hot as he bent over to pick up his books. For the first time he was forced to realize that someone might not like him. It didn't yet occur to him that maybe he needed to toughen up, merely that other people needed to be nicer. This was his first experience with being the sole target of a taunting, older and bigger person. It seemed he always had Sherry or one of his brothers around. He knew now that there would be times that he would have to face bad situations all by himself.

Sherry listened carefully to Larence as he talked quickly and spilled his guts about what happened. When he paused to catch his breath, Sherry was able to get a word in.

"It's gonna be okay Larence. She won't be messing with you anymore. I'm going to take care of things." She hugged him and made sure he had calmed down before she let him go.

As Sherry held Larence in her arms, she heard him sniffle and knew he was upset at his own vulnerability. He wasn't physically hurt, but his pride had been shattered. He knew Jasmine had taken a cheap shot. Sherry knew it too. Jasmine knew it and Sherry was committed to hurting Jasmine the way she had hurt Larence, if not more. Larence was feeling better after telling his big sister about the whole scenario. He knew Sherry wouldn't let anything slide when it came to her family. All bets would be off if you hurt someone she loved. Sherry had butterflies in her stomach thinking about facing down Jasmine Moon tomorrow.

The telephone woke Sherry up from her nap. It was her best friend Kara on the phone. Kara was about the only person who ever called for Sherry, and she called often.

"Are you okay? Why weren't you in school?"

"Yeah, I'm okay I guess. Just wasn't feeling good this morning. You missed me, huh?"

Kara laughed. "Yeah. Duh. I'm calling aren't I?"

It was a typical teen friendship. The girls had their ups and downs, but they always came back together.

"So, are you going to be back at school tomorrow?"

"Yep. I got something I have to take care of," said Sherry. Kara totally ignored Sherry's response.

"What are you wearing?" The girls would sometimes coordinate outfits.

"Jeans and sneakers," said Sherry.

"What!? Why jeans and sneakers? It's Tuesday; we always dress up on Tuesdays."

Sherry proceeded to tell her all about the eventful day Larence had with Jasmine and the reason behind her avoiding the regular Tuesday uniform.

"That bitch," said Kara. "Too bad I don't ride your bus or I would have let her have it the moment I saw her hassle your brother. She's been messin' with you for way too long. Ugh!" Kara was exasperated and wasn't about to stop. "She is such a prejudice pig. You know she wouldn't be such a bitch if you were white, right?"

"I know," said Sherry.

"Remember the time she spit on you? What a dirty piece of white trash!"

Sherry had forgotten about that incident, at least momentarily. Out of all the dirty things someone could do to another, Jasmine had spit on Sherry. It wasn't a confrontation or anything. As a matter of fact, Sherry hadn't troubled Jasmine for a while, at least not to her face. But a few months ago, as Jasmine got off the bus at her house, she spit directly on the top of Sherry's head when she passed her. By the time Sherry realized what happened, the bus doors were closing and they were pulling away. Jasmine was standing outside looking in, laughing like crazy. That moment was perhaps the angriest Sherry had ever been.

Sherry made an excuse to get off the phone, she was tired of being pissed and still wasn't feeling all that great. She knew tomorrow would arrive soon and she wanted to get some rest.

Iceburg

Morning came fast, just like Sherry expected. Fortunately, she had got about 10 hours of sleep and was feeling completely better when her alarm went off. She rolled off the bed to do say her morning prayers, forgetting all of what she was about to face, if only for a moment. She was just saying her amen when Larence's scuffling about the house snapped her out of her zone and back into the reality of the morning. Suddenly all of the anger flooded back to her, seeing Jasmine spitting on her and laughing as the bus pulled away. The bus driver didn't believe her when she tried to tell him what happened and Sherry knew none of the other kids on the bus that day would back her up.

Because Jasmine lived in Desy Cove, even those who weren't racist tended to side with her; she was their neighbor and Sherry was just one-half of a feud they would rather not be involved in. It seemed that the only ones who would speak to her would do so when no one else was looking. Once they got around each other, however, they were like comrades in the same army. Sherry had tried to move on from that humiliating act and take the high road. In a way it was good that Jasmine got off the bus immediately — it gave Sherry a chance to cool off. But deciding not to do anything about the incident seemed to make Jasmine think she had the upper hand. Messing with Larence, though, was the final straw. Sherry didn't care if all of the kids from Desy Cove jumped in to defend Jasmine, and she didn't care about the trouble she would get into at school and at home; Jasmine was going to regret messing with the Sweetstones for a lifetime.

The bus ride to school was quiet and uneventful. It seemed as though the kids knew what happened to Larence, and they all waited in quiet anticipation for retaliation. Sherry was a cool as a cucumber this morning. She remembered what her grandmother said, "Revenge is a dish that is better served cold." Then Sade Sweetstone would say "when you do serve it, make sure it's what you want to feed them and something they really hate to eat." Words to live by, thought Sherry. It was obvious Jasmine didn't know that saying. She got on the bus dressed for the occasion, wearing jeans, sneakers and a sweatshirt. It really was her normal gear, but Sherry noticed Jasmine jumped on the bus with a smirk on her face and with a little more pep than normal. Sherry ignored her. This must have made

Jasmine feel even cockier, thinking that Sherry had backed down and was afraid of her.

"Whatever you do Larence, don't look at Jasmine or Ben Moon," Sherry spoke quietly to her brother. "Just get off the bus and go straight to class like nothing is happening."

Larence did as Sherry told him to. The two were close in age and got even closer because of the adversities they faced at a young age. Things like Jasmine made them very protective of one another. The school day dragged on, and Sherry thought the seventh period class would never end. She had a slight headache from thinking too much about how she would try to handle different scenarios. She was a planner and this was definitely a situation she wanted to be certain to plan all the way out. She tried to discern how things would go down. One thing she knew for sure, she wasn't going to mess around talking to her friends before the bus pulled off like she normally did. She wanted to get on the bus early to make sure Larence was okay. The final bell rang and Sherry hurried to her locker to put her books away. She had homework but decided to travel light and deal with that in the morning.

Her stomach had butterflies and Sherry knew the bus ride wouldn't be pleasant. She realized that Jasmine was tough and that she drew her toughness from a place of anger. Sherry thought for a moment about where that hatred could come from. Something must really bother that girl to make her so hateful. She closed her locker and turned; Kara was waving to her to come down the hall. Sherry shook her head no and screamed "I have to go Kara--call me!" Sherry looked to the exit behind her and darted out before Kara could question her brush off.

When she got outside, she could see the buses lining up, and the fourth one down was bus sixty-seven; that was hers. She took a deep breath and walked towards the bus, the butterflies in her stomach fluttering like their wings were made of iron. Climbing the stairs of the bus, Sherry looked over the rails of the front seat and glanced around for Larence. *Good,* thought Sherry, *Larence isn't on yet.* She found a seat four rows back from the front. She sat on the bus driver's side. It was a substitute driver today and Sherry knew he wouldn't be looking back all the time at the kids like the regular driver Mrs. Downs. The kids thought she had eyes in the back of her head, but it was just a huge rear view mirror and the ability to drive and watch simultaneously. By the way she always knew what was going on, it seemed she kept one eye on the road and one on the kids at all times.

Larence climbed on the bus and looked relieved to see Sherry was on before him. Sherry slid her legs out to let Larence move towards the window seat. Ben Moon popped over the steps and into the aisle, oblivious to Sherry sitting up front and already on the bus. He noticed Sherry and immediately looked around for his sister. No Jasmine. Ben tried to hurry to his seat near the back of the bus. As he got passed Sherry seat he thought he was safe. Sherry casually and quickly stuck out her foot, sliding it backwards so he would think he got past her safely, and then tripped him up. As quickly as she had slid it out, she drew her foot back in so no one would see. He didn't fall and didn't even drop his books, but Sherry got a look at his face and it was obvious that he was both frustrated and embarrassed. Sherry knew it was a cheap shot. She really had no problem with the kid other than he stared at her too much and happened to be Jasmine's brother. Sherry turned back towards the front of the bus, feeling the slightest tinge of guilt for hurting Ben's pride.

Jasmine got on the bus, completely ignoring Sherry. She was at ease, believing that her and Sherry had let things go for now. Jasmine Moon had a lot going on at home, things Sherry could never guess just by looking at her, things that gave her the anger and hate that made her seem so mean and cruel. She was a victim. There was a predator in her home. She didn't act like a tomboy because that's what she liked, she did it hoping that *he* wouldn't. She wanted to be unattractive. The aggressiveness she delivered toward Sherry was out of the hate and low self-esteem she felt about herself. Picking on Sherry made her feel better for a moment. It eased some of the pain and provided a distraction. She really thought Sherry was better than her and thought she could bring her down to her own level by making her miserable too.

Sherry's heart was pounding. She wasn't sure if Ben would tell Jasmine about him getting tripped up by Sherry, but in all honesty she knew it didn't really matter; it wasn't the only thing that would give the Moon kids something to remember this day by.

It didn't take long for Sherry to get confirmation she was waiting for.

Her rear end hung off the seat a little because the seats were too small and Larence always put his book bag on the seat instead of the dirty school bus floor. Sherry felt a pain in her right butt cheek. She had never been kicked in the butt, but she knew immediately what the pain was. She turned around quickly to catch a glimpse of Jasmine going back to her seat. She was fuming. *Typical of the bitch to attack me while my back is turned.* Sherry turned to Larence, "Jasmine just kicked me. I don't know what's going to happen next, but back my play."

Sherry jumped up ran at top speed to the seat were Jasmine and Ben Moon were sitting. Jasmine was sitting closest to the window and Ben was on the aisle. The seat in front of Jasmine's was empty. Sherry quickly slid across it and leaned over the seat. With her knees on the seat in front of the Moons, and her upper body hanging over the back of the seat, Sherry leaned over and without saying a word delivered powerful blow to Jasmine's temple, following it up with an uppercut to her chin. Ben tried defending himself and his sister by hitting Sherry in her chest. Sherry turned to him with a look that said, "you want some?" She hit Ben with her left fist and then turned back to Jasmine with her right fist. Taking turns she sent a left to Ben, a right to Jasmine. Sherry lost her balance as Jasmine tried to stand. She quickly got off the seat and went around, squeezing into Jasmine and Ben's aisle. Jasmine tried to fight back but Sherry was pissed off and felt indestructible. As Ben hit Sherry in the stomach, she didn't feel a thing. Sherry leaned right over Ben kneeling on him as he sat, to get to Jasmine. Jasmine was her focus. She had enough of everything and everyone that hurt her.

All of it came out of her on the bus that day and Jasmine became the recipient of years' worth of anger. Sherry thought back to the time she was jumped in the school-yard at the age of eight by nine boys. It was picture-day and she was wearing her little pink dress and black shoes. She was held in a circle, shoved around like the little silver ball in a pinball machine, tossed this way and that, punched and kicked. She also remembered the look on her racist teacher's face when she put her head down on her desk crying uncontrollably. Looking for comfort from an authority figure, the only thing she got from her teacher was a cold, "you will live." It was like opening up a spigot and being unable to shut it back off-- there was no stopper. Unfortunately it all flooded onto Jasmine Moon.

As Sherry hit her repeatedly, she knew Jasmine had got enough when blood erupted from Jasmine's mouth onto Sherry's coat, splattering on her, Ben and the window next to her. Jasmine fell between the seats. Ben screamed like a little girl; he was terrified to see his big sister, his role model, go down like a limp rag. Sherry also went into a zone unknown to her. When she saw that Jasmine had fallen, she instantly stopped. She calmly pushed herself off of Ben's body and went back to her seat.

Everyone on the bus was astounded; they had never seen anything like it. A girl half Jasmine's size kicking the crap out of her and her brother. The substitute driver was half-clueless to the fight, screaming, "What's going on back there? Break it up!"

As Sherry settled back in her seat, she felt hot and overwhelmed with emotions. She had to stop herself from crying. Not because she was hurt, but because she was upset. She didn't feel the way she thought she would by beating up on Jasmine and Ben. She was overcome with guilt and sadness. That initial release-- the relief she felt to get all of that anger out of her-- was replaced with regret. She felt horrible and knew she was in big trouble. Not just with the school, but when she got home her father would be fuming.

Sherry and Larence got off the bus. The phone began ringing before Sherry and Larence got all the way into the house. "Don't answer it," she calmly told Larence. It would be Kara on the other end and she didn't feel like talking. A few hours later, the phone rang again. This time it was the school. Mr. and Mrs. Sweetstone got the news that one of their children was fighting on the bus and was not welcome back on for three days. As her father talked on the phone, Sherry was sure she would get a whoopin' that night. He got off the phone and turned slowly to her.

"Sit down," he said motioning to the table. Sherry sat, scared to death of her father's icy stare.

She began to explain the entire situation, from the day that confrontations with Jasmine began to her hassling Larence. When she was finished, she looked at her father, who sat in silence. She lowered her head, afraid to look him in the face. When he broke the silence, she was shocked at what he had to say.

"Well I guess you did what you had to. Next time you need to tell us what's going on before it gets to this point though," he said sternly. "And maybe next time you can back off before the other kid starts bleeding like a stuck pig." He shook his head, but she thought she saw the corners of his mouth turn up slightly as he looked away.

Sherry's dad was proud of her. He knew what his kids had to endure and though he wasn't the type to welcome negative attention, he also didn't want them to swallow their pride and put up with the mistreatment. They had to stand up for themselves if they wanted to earn respect.

Because the school was twenty-five minutes by bus from the house and both of Sherry's parents worked and couldn't take her, she got the next three days off. It was exactly what she needed, a break from the children of Desy Cove. It was too good to be true. Her father wasn't upset and she was home from school.

The break gave her a lot of time to think. It was the first night of her suspension, as she laid in bed thinking about the fight that she remembered a dream she had about fighting on a bus years before. It was happening more and more that something would happen and it would trigger the memory of a dream from years prior. Sherry didn't understand what was happening; it was like her life was reaffirming the thoughts she had dreamt. Sometimes it took a few months for the dream to come to fruition, and other times it took years. Though she wasn't completely clear on the how or why of it, she hoped to one day. She also struggled to understand why people would pick on her because of the way she looked. She still didn't hate white people for their skin, even though they treated her as an outsider.

"Jay-Jay," a voice whispered in the dark. That was Jasmine's nickname given to her by her family. Jasmine immediately knew the voice and the tone of

deception. She was lying in bed, in the fetal position, licking her wounds with an ice bag on her lips.

"Are you ok sweetie? I heard what happened; let me see."

Jasmine rolled over and let her father see her face. He kissed her forehead softly. She could smell the alcohol on his breath. She hoped with everything in her that this time his attention would be genuine, that this time he actually cared about his daughter being hurt at school and wouldn't take advantage of her vulnerability. He removed the ice bag gently from Jasmine face, and replaced it with his hand, gently touching her sore lips. Then he slowly kissed her. Jasmine turned her face to the side, sick with anticipation, afraid and utterly alone.

Her father whispered, "Now, now Jay, you know you love your daddy don't you? I just want to dry your tears and make you feel better. "He turned her face back towards him, placed his hands around her back and held her close to him. He hugged his hairy arms around her began rubbing on her back. Jasmine tried to push herself free, but it was too late. Mr. Moon slipped himself on top off Jasmine, pinning her to the bed. She knew what was about to happen; it had happened so many times before. There was nothing she could do. She froze. And the tears ran down her face, as she tried to remember the last time she didn't feel like taking her life

Chapter 3
—Extended-Family—

Come on, come on! It feels like we'll never get home. Sherry was on the bus watching the snow-covered ground whizz by outside. School had been uneventful. Everyone had heard about the fight on the bus and Sherry didn't think she would be dealing with any bullies for the remainder of her time at Centennial Elementary. She figured Larence would be safe too. She thought hopefully that her new reputation might just follow her all the way to high school.

The country road was clear, but the leafless maple and oak trees still had snow hanging on their branches. She could hear the sound of the logs dropping to the ground from the lumber mill. Sherry was close to home.

Sherry could not get the memory of last night's dream out of her mind. In it she had seen Larence out on the frozen Severn River in danger. Knowing her history of dreams, she had said a prayer the moment she opened her eyes. *God please don't let anything happen to my brother Larence.* That was when she heard her father's truck barreling up the driveway, providing a distraction from the nightmare.

She wanted to tell her best friend Kara about her dreams, but hadn't yet gotten the courage and decided just to keep this one a secret too. She wasn't sure Kara, or anyone else for that reason, would believe her.

It was Feburary, ice skating season, and she knew Kara would want her to get out on the river with her. She was leery of getting on the frozen river every year and this year would be no different. She knew Kara would pressure her to get out there before she was ready; that was just how Kara was.

Kara Lemon was Sherry's best friend and she was very persistent. Persistent was a nice way of putting it—Kara was spoiled. She always got her way at home and saw no reason that her social life should be any different. Her parents had a little money, and although they were going through a divorce, or maybe *because* they were going through a divorce, they let Kara run wild and get anything she wanted. She was a little on the chunky side with ghostly skin and hair to match. She was average-- some days she looked cute, but her personality was very mean and conniving. Her mother blamed her meanness on her birth parents. Kara was adopted. To many, attitude made her ugly. Many of the kids in River Sades kept their distance because they knew Kara couldn't be trusted. Sherry sighed; doubtful she would be able to hold Kara off any longer. Kara had been on her about getting on the ice for about a week and Sherry was running out of excuses.

The bus finally stopped across the street from Sherry's long driveway. As she climbed off, she could hear King and Queeny barking there heads of for some reason. The faithful family pets usually were calm unless there was an intruder close by. In the distance walking down River Sades Boulevard, was Mrs. Carolyn Knight and her vicious dog Lightning. King ran across the street to greet Sherry and Larence.

King & Queeny

"Think she'll be alright?" said a seven-year old Sherry to Maurice as they both backed their heads out of Queeny's dog house.

"Go get mom," said Maurice. "I'll make sure she stays warm."

They both stared at Queeny panting and giving birth to her seventh pup. "Go now Sherry!"

The pups were still coming when Sherry returned. Maurice petted his favorite dog in the world and kept the blankets close to her. Mrs. Sweetstone arrived carrying a box and a basin of warm water. She was a stout woman with gray and black hair. Her timeless face held her glasses. Mrs. Sweetstone was a hard working woman with hands to prove it. She had seen a lot in her time, but remained humble and generally happy. She also had a love for pets, especially stray ones.

Queeny showed up five years ago in a rain storm, when Sherry was just five. She escaped from the hands of animal control, after living on her own for several weeks in the woods behind Perch Run Road. The night of a particularly bad storm, Queeny was foraging in the woods when lightning struck a tree. A branch fell out of the sky, barely missing her and just clipping her tail. The impact scared the dog and she bolted, running and looking for shelter. The next morning, Mrs. Sweetstone found her on the front porch. She had curled up in a ball under the awning and was sleeping soundly when Mrs. Sweetstone opened the front door to come out and feed her stray tom cat, the one she swore was friends with the local raccoons.

The Sweetstones had a large screened in porch, pretty typical for out in the country. And outside of the screened-in area, there was a landing and several steps to the front yard. As Mrs. Sweetstone walked out onto the porch, she began calling the cat. She walked across the porch and saw something brown in front of the door. She tried to push open the door and it would not budge. Suddenly Queeny awoke from the force of the door. She sat up quickly with her big brown eyes and her caramel coat, and immediately ran down into the yard. It's always hard to tell with strays, but Mrs. Sweetstone said that Queeny was half German Shepard and half Collie.

"Hey girl you hungry?" said Sadie Sweetstone in her gentle voice. She opened the screen door and shook the bowl of cat food, laying it down in front of her feet. Queeny wasted no time and ran onto the porch to eat. It was gone so fast Mrs. Sweetstone had no time to give Queeny a once-over. She knew from experience that strays were often injured, whether from other animals or former owners. She hurried into the house to get plastic bowels, filling one with leftovers and the other with cold water.

"Take your time girl; no one is going to take it from you." She petted Queeny while she ate to test her manners. Queeny looked up from her dish, cocked her head to the side, and went back to eating. Mrs. Sweetstone knew she had a friend. Dogs with behavioral issues aren't too keen on being petted while eating and Mrs. Sweetstone knew this dog was special and would be safe around her children. If the two developed a trust early-on, she could also be protective of the home and the people within.

Mrs. Sweetstone looked Queeny over and saw she was injured. She quickly dug out some old rags from a basket on the porch and bandaged Queeny up. You need a name, said Mrs. Sweetstone looking at her new dog. Since you sit up so straight and proud said Mrs. Sweetstone I'll call you Queeny. Queeny waged her tail giving approval. Sitting on the screened-in porch, Mrs. Sweetstone looked at her sanctuary. To the right were her pet birds and a house mouse that she didn't have the heart to kill. She knew Queeny would be a good addition, as the only thing they were missing was a good watch dog. Of course she would have to live outside, both of the Sweetstone parents but especially Red were from the old school and believed pets don't belong in a house.

Every time it stormed, from that day on, Queeny would make a dash to try to get into the house. When that didn't work, she would run into River Sades and one of the neighbors would feel sorry for her. Recognizing she was the Sweetstone dog, they would give her shelter until the storm passed. Back then dogs could run through neighborhoods without people freaking out when they saw one not wearing a collar. Everyone knew everybody's pet within the five mile radius. Queeny was well-known and liked everywhere. She warded off strangers trying to come onto the Sweetstone property and alerted the family with a healthy bark. Only when she heard, "no barking" would she stop. She was a well-mannered dog. But when it came to protecting her young she did not hold back-- she could tear you to shreds.

She became very protective of Sherry and her brothers, following them everywhere they went and waiting outside to walk them home. Sometimes she would meet the children when they came home from a friends or got off the bus, standing at the end of the long driveway waiting for them. She was smart. She traveled on the opposite side of the road as if she was a hiker and always looked both ways before crossing the street. She taught her puppies to do the same. Because Queeny had lived in the woods there were times she went off to chase old demons and clear her head from the tortured life she once had. She wouldn't come home until dark. Sometimes she would be gone for days at a time, but the Sweetstones knew she would return and she would leave her then-grown pups to guard the place in her absence.

Mrs. Sweetstone gently wiped the pups clean with a wash rag and warm water. Then she placed them gently against Queeny to nurse. Sherry was excited to see them being born. A few of the pups were still born because there were simply so many. Mrs. Sweetstone calmed Sherry down and showed her how to rub them gently to stimulate breathing. The pups would begin moving and let out a faint gasp and cry. Sherry was thrilled and relieved.

"Thank you God!" She yelled out like she and her mother had just carried out a miracle. Sherry had inherited her mother's love for pets.

There were thirteen puppies this year and Sherry wanted to keep them all. Maurice, Sherry and Larence got to pick out two pups, both males. The rest were given away. As the puppies were given to new homes, one by one, Sherry felt a pain in her gut for Queeny having to say goodbye to her children. The two boys that stayed behind were named King and Shirt. The disappointment of seeing the other pups go soon subsided, however, as all of their free time seemed to be spent running around with the two bundles of joy they got to keep.

King was the biggest off the litter and Shirt was the runt. King was all-white and looked like a full-blooded German Shepard. Raised with Queeny's expertise, they were both very well behaved dogs. Queeny seemed to be glad to get some help patrolling the property at night; it was a lot of ground to cover. Shirt was Larence's dog; they took to each other right away. The little orange and white runt had a spot of black on his side. He followed Larence everywhere. Shirt earned his name when Larence shouted out, "Look at his colors, he looks like he is wearing a shirt!" Eventually he grew up to look similar to a beagle. If no one had told you, you would have never guessed the dogs came from the same litter.

Lightning

"Go home King!" yelled Sherry as her heart began to race. She saw Mrs. Knight and Lightning getting closer and she was hoping King wouldn't spot them. The kids hurried towards King who had walked up the driveway to greet them. Larence grabbed him with both arms; he seldom wore a collar.

"C'mon King. Let's go." Larence began to turn King around, but the dog had something else in mind. He broke free from Larence's grasp. He danced in the street, pacing back and forth bidding Lighten to join him.

Though his tail wagged when Lightning was far enough away, Sherry knew the two dogs hated one another. Lightning was a mean-spirited dog who thought he ran the neighborhood. Seeing King, Lightning broke free from the side of Mrs. Knight and tore down the street.

Mrs. Knight, carrying a big stick, raised it in the air shouting, "Lightning get back here!" Aside from the yelling, she made little actual effort to *do* anything, which wasn't abnormal when it came to her control over her dog. Lightning was vicious. Though King had learned to spar from the best, his mother Queeny, he was no match for the older and scrappier dog.

As the two dogs got within a foot of one another, Larence and Sherry stepped back. They both feared Lightning and were secretly hoping King would win the battle. While they both were willing to jump in and help King, they knew from raising him that sooner or later he would have to earn his stripes. Today he was ready, and it seemed he wouldn't back down this time. They circled each other in the street. The tension was thick, until Lightning broke it by pouncing on King, going for his neck. King broke free, came up on his hind legs, and the two went at each other with more determination than ever before. Though it was King's first real dog fight, you couldn't tell. Lightning, however, had been around the block.

Sherry's eyes started to tear up as she screamed to Mrs. Knight to call off her dog. Mrs. Knight seemed to be getting satisfaction as her dog proved to overpower King. King let out a yelp. Queeny, who was resting near the house, heard the cry of her first-born. She quickly bolted towards the sound of her son. She stood at the top off the embankment of the driveway and saw her neighborhood enemy, Lightning. She let out a growl. King, hearing his mother, got a boost of confidence and went at Lightning again. Queeny growled again and King stopped immediately, as if his mother was saying, "Kid, step aside."

She came off the hillside crawling low on her belly and sideways like a reptile. She knew the nature of this beast that she was dealing with. Lightning had been a thorn in Queeny's side for years. He usually knew to keep his distance. She was twice his age, and Lightning coward at the sight of her. But that wasn't enough for Queeny; he had crossed a line by coming to her home and messing with her son.

Queeny quickly pounced on him, taking several bites out of him and then holding his neck to the ground. Mrs. Knight shouted, "Get your dog!" But Sherry and Larence ignored her. She pleaded, "Get your goddamn dog!"

Sherry turned to Larence, "Take King and go home." The bus was coming back through, finishing the route. Sherry shouted, "Queen, go home girl."

Within an instant, Queeny let Lightning go. Mrs. Knight ran over towards Sherry.

"You kids need to control your dog!"

"You always walk that mean dog without a leash, our dogs were just protecting their territory." Sherry knew better than to talk back to an adult, but she had grown tired of Lightning and his owner. As soon as she finished her sentence, she bolted across the street to her house, hoping that Lightning's behavior would justify her words.

"Good girl," she said to Queeny. "You are the prettiest and smartest dog in the world." Sherry was proud of Queeny, There was something about the dog's instinct to protect and standup for Sherry and Larence while they were in danger. Sherry and Larence didn't see that coming and really had no idea Queeny had that kind of fight in her. Sherry loved her dog even more after that day. She loved her so much, it pained her heart.

Shirt

"Shirt! Shirt!" called Larence as he stepped out on the porch to feed his dog. He stepped over Queeny and the tomcat. Larence was nervous. He had a bad feeling when his dog wasn't on the porch waiting to be fed every morning. Shirt was a creature of habit and one of the habits he excelled at was eating. Like clockwork, he would be at the front door waiting on his food. This particular morning, however, Larence didn't see him anywhere.

Iceburg

As he stood there calling Shirt, Larence remembered last night hearing a car skidding on the dirt road. He didn't think anything of it at the time, but this morning the memory made him sick to his stomach. He took off running towards the road. As Larence reached the edge of the driveway, his heart started racing and he began to fear the worst. Larence looked left and then right on Perch Run Road. In the distance toward the lumber yard, about a thousand feet away, he could see something lying in the road. He ran as fast as he could, yelling for his dog Shirt. Tears started rolling down his face even before he got close enough to see him. But there was no mistaking the little dog lying lifeless in the road. He kneeled over Shirt and began to sob uncontrollably, "Noooo…God. No not Shirt!" Larence heard a whimper; he knew it wasn't coming from Shirt. He looked towards the woods and saw King lying near the side of the road, on his belly with his head resting on his paws, watching Larence. For a moment, Larence was relieved that Shirt didn't die alone. King didn't leave his brother's side. The two must have been out hunting that as in earlier morning, thought Larence, and tried to cross the road to head home.

"Good Boy!" Larence gently said to King. He wiped the tears from his eyes. He was glad to see King alive and was proud of the dog for sitting there with his brother all night. Larence took off his coat and picked up Shirt, gently wrapping him in it.

Larence took the path home as King followed. Looking around for a good place to bury Shirt, he found their favorite spot up on Mount Everest were all the kids played stick-it pick-it. Over the hillside there was a beautiful valley where the deer grazed. Larence laid Shirt down, still wrapped up in his coat and raced home to get Sherry.

"Sherry!" screamed Larence as he got close to the house. "Come quick!" Sherry jumped up from the breakfast table and ran outside to the sound of Larence's voice.

"What's going on Larence?" As he stood catching his breath, he began to cry again.

"Shirt got hit by a stupid car; I found him dead in the road by the lumber yard." Sherry held out her arms and embraced her little brother as he sobbed. Sherry hadn't really been close to Shirt, but she knew Larence loved that little dog and his sobs brought her to tears.

They took off walking as Larence explained where he wanted to bury Shirt. Sherry grabbed a shovel from her father's shed on their way. They walked for about a mile, reminiscing about Shirt and how funny and loving he was. Larence felt better talking to Sherry and he maintained his composure. She convinced him that his dog was in a better place, at home with many other dogs running free! They reached Mount Everest. As they climbed the hillside, Sherry felt badly for Larence, knowing how he would miss his best friend. She vowed to give special attention to her little brother. When they reached the bundle, Sherry unwrapped it to have a look. Shirt looked peaceful. Sherry thought he must have had internal injuries because he didn't look too bad.

Sherry started digging while Larence sat and watched. Normally, she would have put him to work too, but this time was different. She gently lifted Shirt and placed him in the ground. Fighting back the tears, Sherry said a prayer "Lord thank you for our time with Shirt. We are grateful and we will see him again one day. Amen."

"Amen," whispered Larence and he began pushing dirt over his dog's body. The two found old pieces of wood and made a cross marking his resting place. "See ya Shirt," said Larence, and they started back down the mountain.

Chapter 4
Mount Everest

It was late summer of 1979 and Sherry had just turned twelve. The anticipation of another rite of passage stayed on her mind. The hundreds of acres surrounding the Sweetstone home created a recipe for adventure and the cooler weather meant it was time to take the long hike to Everest. Everyone between the ages of 11 and 17 came migrating out of River Sades on that cool sunny day. As Maurice looked out the window he could see his friends. All of the Barnes children including Pete's youngest and only sister Bernadette, who Sherry had met a few years back and they became best friends.

"Hurry up," said Maurice to Sherry and Larence. "Grab those boxes," he said pointing to a stack on the porch. Larence was not really at the age to be hiking to Everest with the other kids, but he got to go by default since the shortcut was on the Sweetstone property. All of the Sweetstone kids felt that the woods surrounding their home was their personal playground and the others from River Sades were trespassing, unless they had been given permission by a member of the Sweetstone family. Besides, Maurice didn't go too many places without his little brother, who idolized his every move.

The three of them ran up the path to intercept the other kids from River Sades, exchanging hellos. Bernadette and Sherry paired up right away, catching up about their summer adventures. Soon it would be time to go back to school. The two didn't really discuss why they hadn't hung out that much over the summer; they never did. It was clear to Sherry that Bernadette didn't like being around Kara. It was something that didn't have to be said. It was obvious. And Sherry didn't mind that. With Kara, everything seemed to be a popularity contest or a fight, especially as they had gotten older. While Kara seemed to get more and more of an attitude, Sherry got less and less interested in her friendship. With Bernadette, everything was laid back. Though they would go months without talking, they were always able to pick up where they left off.

Bernadette Barnes was very pretty with long dirty-blonde hair that she wore feathered back, and blue eyes. To the boys, she was one of the catches of the neighborhood. That was, if you could catch her. Bernadette had a perfect slim body that was developing well compared with many of the girls their age. She was very soft spoken and had five brothers which made it a little more difficult for the boys to get at her. Five brothers made a formidable security system, challenging any little boy that would come near the youngest and only girl in the Barnes family. She was very athletic, but unlike Sherry, she was no tomboy; she was a girly girl.

Sherry looked up at the sky; she could feel an awesome day coming. The trees had lost most of their leaves, and with the tall white oaks showing their bare branches, it looked like it snowed. Looking into the distance, she could see hundreds of tall pines standing high up on the mountain. Some of the maple and poplar trees still had their orange and yellow leaves. But down here in the low lands, the ground was covered and the leaves crunched underfoot as they walked. Sherry thought to herself, I'm glad we don't have to rake the woods.

Sherry was overjoyed because she was finally invited to go with the group to Everest. She was no longer viewed as being too young by Maurice and his friends, and that meant they wouldn't treat her like she was in the way or an annoyance. Truly, Sherry knew it meant that she was old enough to see what they did and not tell. Sherry had been to Everest a few times before the Boy Scouts discovered it.

As they got to the foot of the mountain, all fifteen kids gathered at the stream and took a cold drink of water using their hands. *It was great to rough it,* thought Sherry as she looked around at everyone doing their own thing. *No rules, no adults, just us teenagers taking care of ourselves.* Everest

Iceburg

was freedom at its best. And when you get to the top, adults have no clue where you are.

"Everybody ready to go up?" Pete said, being the natural leader. As Sherry looked up toward where they were headed she noticed there were steps built into the mountain side. There was a piece of maple about every three feet. This eased any apprehensions she had about making the climb.

"Who put in the steps?" Sherry asked her older brother Maurice.

"Me and the guys did," he responded with a pleased look on his face. Back then, being a Boy Scout was something to be proud of, not teased over. And Maurice was definitely proud of himself. Sherry had been to Everest a few times, but that was with the whole family and before the Boy Scouts discovered it, definitely before the steps.

This was going to be an easier climb, thought Sherry. In the past the hike was grueling, constantly trying to keep your footing and slipping a little all the way up. But it was worth it, she did remember that. On this day, as they climbed, Sherry would look down for minutes at a time then look up, hoping to see a difference in the distance to the top. But that distance didn't seem to change fast enough at all. Looking up, it seemed that the climb would take forever. But, about an hour later the teenagers reached the top. A few of the guys beat on their chest, screaming like Tarzan, Sherry's brothers included. Sherry looked at Bernadette and rolled her eyes at the boys until Bernadette grabbed her by the hands and began to spin her around until they both got dizzy and fell to the ground laughing. Whether it was the thinner air or the exhaustion from the climb, everyone seemed to be in really high spirits.

"I'm gonna go check out the new camp," Bernadette said to Sherry. The Boy Scouts had built a new campsite on the mountain earlier in the summer. "Wanna come?" she asked.

"Nah go ahead. I'm gonna stay here," responded Sherry.

Sherry stood up, dusted off her butt and took in the view. She closed her eyes letting the cool breeze and sun hit her face. When she opened her eyes Sherry could see for miles. She loved the view from the top of Everest. That's what the kids named it after learning about one of the tallest mountains in the world in school. They thought since we can't go there in person. Let's pretend when we're hiking. We will imagine were climbing Mount Everest. While their hill was just that, a large hill, they had since referred to it as "the mountain" or just Everest.

As Sherry turned to get the full view, she caught one particular sight that made the hair on the back of her neck stand up. Sherry stared at the white and gray mansion on the hill west of Everest. It had a perfectly manicured lawn and white picket fence that went on for acres. All along the ten-acre plot were No Trespassing signs. You could only get a clear view of the house in the fall. Any other time, you would have to work up the courage to step your feet on the grounds. The Whittnore Farm gave Sherry the creeps. She swore that even if it weren't for the stories she had heard, she would think the place looked haunted.

The Whittnore Mansion

As Sherry had heard it from her parents and even grandparents, the house was built in the early 1900's by Jester Whittnore, who ran a tobacco plantation. The place was thriving in the early years, and when he passed, he left the operation to his son. Sebastian Whittnore went off to war, leaving his wife home alone with the field workers. It was rumored that his wife carried on with one of the field hands and got pregnant. When Mr. Whittnore came home from the war and discovered his wife pregnant, he knew it wasn't his-- he had been gone too long. He was understandably furious. Eventually his wife, Mrs. Lovie Whittnore, confessed that she had been messing around because she was lonely and wanted attention. She begged for Mr. Whittnore's forgiveness. Instead, in his grief and shame, Mr. Whittnore locked her in the basement, in a room off the right wing of the mansion. That night she supposedly gave birth to the baby in a rocking chair. Mr. Whittnore ignored the screams of the baby and his wife; he sealed off the room with boards and left them both to die. The stories say that mother and child have been there ever since and that the door to the room still doesn't open. Many families have come and went from the Whittnore property.

Sherry was too young to remember, but her mother told her that many years ago, when Sherry was about two and Larence was a baby, she

Iceburg

had cleaned for a woman that lived there. Ms. Noble was a widow whose husband died of a heart attack shortly after moving into the mansion. Ms. Noble had told Mrs. Sweetstone that he had died in the basement as he went to investigate a noise he heard. As he placed his hand on the doorway to the sealed room, he clutched his chest and died instantly. The rumor was that he had heard the child crying.

Ms. Noble owned two white German shepherds. One day while Mrs. Sweetstone was cleaning, Ms. Noble went out for the day. In her absence, the two dogs started howling and went to the basement. There they paced back and forth in front of the locked door. Then they started scratching at it. Mrs. Sweetstone, frightened to death but not wanting to have Ms. Noble to come home to anything unexpected, went down the steps slowly to see what the dogs were up to. There, as she stood on the steps to the basement, she heard a baby crying. She knew Larence and Sherry were both upstairs napping while she worked and that there were no other children there. A sick feeling in her gut told her to not go any further. On that instinct she backed up slowly on the staircase, climbing backwards until she reached the main floor. Then, she quickly grabbed her kids and hauled ass towards the front door. She could still hear the dogs howling. Right as she reached the front door Ms. Noble walked in.

"You startled me, "said Mrs. Sweetstone, trying to catch her breath and appear calm.

"Are you okay dear?" said Ms. Noble as she could see the ghostly look on Mrs. Sweetstone's face.

"Well, truthfully, no. Your dogs are barking frantically in the basement."

"Oh! That again," said Ms. Noble, obviously having dealt with the issue before. "Are they barking at the door?"

"Yes, as far as I can tell," said Mrs. Sweetstone.

Ms. Noble looked down at her shoes, lifting her eyes up to meet Mrs. Sweetstones and said, "I believe my house is a bit haunted."

A bit? thought Sherry's mother. *Any "bit" of haunting is enough.*

"When we first bought the house--meaning my husband and I--we were told that the door in the basement wouldn't open and to not try and open it. Of course we ignored the warning and tried to take it down, but it wouldn't budge."

Mrs. Sweetstone noticed she was no longer hearing the baby crying, but she still wanted to get out of the house, and Ms. Noble's story wasn't helping settle her fears.

"Whenever we tried to mess with the door, the basement would get so cold, like there was a window open in the winter," Ms. Noble went on. "But despite all the weird happenings we loved this old mansion so much that we couldn't see ourselves leaving." She looked at Mrs. Sweetstone like she wanted some kind of assurance that her desire to stay in the creepy old house was understandable.

I guess you want to leave in a box like your husband, Mrs. Sweetstone thought to herself. She smiled slightly and said, "I see."

The next day she called Ms. Noble and quit. The final straw came in speaking with her mother-in-law, who told her that she had worked for the original Mr. Whittnore Sr. Leon and Shirley Sweetstone worked on the tobacco farm for years when it was rumored that Mrs. Whittnore took sick and was in the suite off the basement recuperating. No one knew the truth at the time. Shirley Sweetstone and her husband were among the few staff members that weren't let go when Mr. Whittnore had returned from fighting in the war. The tobacco farm was thriving, but he was getting more difficult to work for. The rumor was he had lost his mind watching his young and vibrant wife get weak and ill. Little did everyone know, he had let her die of starvation while locked in the basement.

Shirley was housekeeping in the absence of Mrs. Whittnore and was told to stay out of the basement at all costs. In those days you didn't ask questions you just did as you were told to keep food on the table. Early one morning Leon and Shirley arrived for work and Shirley went into the mansion to start cleaning. Leon was planning on painting the shutters. He went into the shed, grabbed his paint and brush, and grabbed the old wooden ladder from beside the cellar door. He leaned the ladder against the house, and as he climbed he noticed a window was open. Through the screen he could hear a woman softly singing, "hush little baby don't you cry," and the creaking of a rocking chair going back and forth. As Leon passed the window, he looked through the screen he saw a room decorated like a nursery. There was a hand-carved maple crib with a white and green quilt folded at the foot. On it he saw the name Sam embroidered. The room was a lime green with crown molding around the ceiling and wooden alphabet letters hung throughout. He didn't recall the Whittnores having any children. Leon about fell off the ladder when he noticed the aged woman with white hair bared a striking resemblance to Mrs. Whittnore. It had to be her mother, thought Leon, this woman has to be at least sixty-years old. "Good Morning!" said Leon, swallowing his fear and breaking the song. Suddenly the chair stopped rocking and the old lady and baby disappeared. Leon let out a scream for his wife and the ladder went falling backwards. Fortunately he didn't have that far to fall and jumped when it got close to the ground. As Leon sat on the ground, still frightened from the haunting sight, Shirley ran to his side.

"What's going on!?" she yelled. He pointed at the window in silence. Shirley took the ladder and leaned it against the window, not quite sure what he was motioning for.

"I think I know why we don't see Mrs. Whittnore no more," he said to his wife.

"What are you talking about Leon?" said Shirley.

"She's dead," said Leon. "And I just seen her ghost."

The two had heard chatter that Mr. Whittnore had killed her or had locked her away, but they assumed it was nothing more than a rumor. Leon explained exactly what he had seen and his loyal wife believed every word, but she wanted to see for herself.

"Come on Leon, look with me," she said as she put her first foot on the ladder. Leon began to climb after her, scared to death but wanting to prove to himself and his wife that he was not losing his mind.

When they reached the open window, they peered in through the screen. The chair was still there, though no one was in it, and it was rocking at top speed. Shirley reached down and grabbed Leon's hand to stop herself from passing out.

Everyone in River Sades and surrounding areas had similar stories about the Whittnore place. Sherry remembered her friend Mathew and his sister

Rebecca who had lived there for a short time. Mathew Van Garlum was seated next to Sherry in her third-grade class. He came in the middle of the year, a good-looking rich kid with light brown hair and green eyes. He wore a long sleeve dress shirt and tie on his first day. Sherry remembered how Mathew always looked tired, and was very shy. He was very mature for their age and reminded Sherry of a little businessman. They became friends whenever they were called to divide up for assignments, or when they had to lineup alphabetically. They were usually next to each other in line because their names were closest in the alphabet. On the bus ride to school, Sherry still sat with Larence and Mathew would sit with his sitter Rebecca. But many mornings Mathew would not be at the bust stop. On those days he would show up late to school. After a while, he missed the bus and never showed back up to school.

Two weeks went by when the bus stopped at the mansion again and two strange looking children got on. Sherry didn't recognize them. The little girl's hair was all white. The boy's hair had streaks of gray throughout. Sherry stared at them as they got on; then the boy turned his head towards Sherry and her heart skipped a beat. It was her friend Mathew. He looked like he was in a trance as he gave Sherry a dismal smile. Sherry lifted her hand slowly to wave at Mathew, wondering if anyone else noticed this ghost sitting on the school bus. When they got to class she drilled Mathew on his whereabouts of the last two weeks. Mathew said he had been sick, that he been sick a lot since he moved to town and that his parents were having a hard time getting along. He told Sherry that he might have to go live with his father. Mathew told Sherry he had a secret to tell her. He made her swear to keep it quiet. But before he could spill the beans, Mrs. Hardhart interrupted him with the day's lesson and a stern "Shhh!"

The next day when the bus stopped at the white and gray mansion, there was no Mathew. Sherry waited impatiently for her friend to come through the classroom door. He never came through the door and Sherry never saw him again. She thought of him often, though and always wondered what his secret was.

Iceburg

"Gotcha!" said James Barnes grabbing Sherry's waist and snapping her back to reality. Sherry screamed and jumped about ten feet high. James Barnes had a crush on Sherry, but the feeling was not mutual. Over the summer he had started picking on her and giving her all this attention. She wasn't entirely sure how to handle it.

"Dang James, leave me alone!" Sherry said exasperated.

Later that day she went deep into the woods to go pee. That what was the girls had to do so the boys couldn't see them. On her way back out, she headed towards the sound of the other kids' laughter. Out of nowhere popped James Barnes. Sherry screamed again. "Did you see me go to the bathroom?"

"No! I swear," said James. He was standing a little too close for Sherry's comfort when he grabbed her and stuck his tongue down her throat. Sherry gasped, disgusted at her slimy first kiss, and pushed him off of her. James started laughing and Sherry, too flustered to say anything, took off running.

She reached her friend Bernadette who was standing on the edge of the group, but was too embarrassed to tell her what happened.

"Where you been?" said Bernadette, not pausing to allow Sherry to answer. "Did you see who just winked at me?"

Sherry was grateful that Bernadette's interest in where she had been was insincere; she didn't feel like having to dance around what had just happened in the woods with James, Bernadette's brother. Sherry searched the small crowd and saw Vince Monkton smiling at Bernadette as if he swallowed a canary. Vince was Bernadette's crush; she had it for him bad. She talked about him constantly and seemed to seriously exaggerate his attention for her, making it out to be more than what it was. Bernadette didn't like the guys her age, and Vince was older. She considered herself very mature. Richard Rondowski wanted to marry Bernadette, or so he proclaimed every time he saw her. He was nice, and cute, but Bernadette was not interested. Vince was the only guy for her. He was four years older, which to him made her jail bait.

Vince and Victor Monkton were brothers. Both were very funny and good looking. They were always tan, even in winter, with long, shaggy dark brown hair and beautiful brown eyes. Vince was the oldest and seemed to be every girl's ideal boyfriend. He was very sweet and attentive and he was quite the show-off. Vince and Pete were an explosive combination. Victor, the younger brother, looked up to his brother and clearly wanted to be like him. Vince picked on Victor a lot, like most older brothers do. They wrestled all the time and were constantly butting heads. Whenever Vince was around, Victor got no attention from the girls. Sherry and Victor were one year apart and good friends. Victor was smart when it came to camping. He was very reliable and mature. You could trust his word. What made Vince and Victor Monkton really popular in River Sades was that they were the biggest stoners you'd ever meet. Vince always had the best pot, or so Sherry heard. So did Victor because he stole it from Vince. Vince not only had great pot but could get ahold of alcohol whenever he needed it. This contributed to his popularity in a major way and also made him a bit of a bad boy.

Maurice, Larence and Pete, with the rest of the gang, were already taking advantage of Everest's pleasures. They had broken the cardboard boxes that the Sweetstones had brought from home down to their original state. With the boxes laid flat, the boys dove their bodies on top of them, using them like sleds. They tried every position possible, on their stomachs, backs, and sitting backwards, while sledding down one short side of the mountain. They did it over and over again, screaming with laughter. Sherry flattened her box and sat cross-legged and Bernadette gave her a push. Down she went, wrapping the edge of the box around her legs to give better control as she zoomed past trees, dodging them like a pro. Now, Sherry knew the one hour climb was worth it. Just to sled halfway down the mountain, her heart raced and she felt true joy rise inside of her. She knew anyone could see her smiling like a Cheshire cat on her way down, and she didn't care.

Dale and Dick Andres were the "stick it pick" kings. So when Pete Barnes yelled for the game to start, Dale and Dick were the first to call being team captains. Pete pulled his screwdriver out from his back pocket and threw it perfectly against the foot of the tall oak tree landing it between its roots.

"Okay, you two start picking your teams," he said.

Dale looked at his younger brother, "Age before beauty," he laughed and began scanning the crowd for who he wanted to select.

The two divided the teams up evenly, choosing the oldest of the kids to the youngest. Maurice was a hot shot for his age, very athletic. However being around the older teenagers and seeing them get chosen before him, he realized there were other good athletes besides him and it taught him patience and a little humility. As the older sibling, it was a hard lesson to wait his turn, but one that needed to be learned. It was when he and his brothers and Sherry were with the other kids that he knew there is always someone better at something that you think you're good at.

Of course Pete made it a point to nudge Dale, so he would choose Dominique Wood. Pete and Dominique disappeared a lot that day, thought Sherry when she saw Pete nudge Dale. The two had a blast sharing a box-sled, Dominique sitting on Pete's lap as they went sliding down the mountain. At times they looked glued together, thought Sherry as she watched Dominique put her hand on Pete's waist as she walked by him to join her team. Sherry didn't see this one coming, but she knew it was just a matter of time; Pete was quite a catch. The boys would tease Dominique because of her last name. They would say "Dominique Wood, would what?" and the boys would fill in the blank with whatever raunchy idea that would come to their mind.

Dominique was a natural glamour girl, beautiful from head to toe. She would wear her skimpy two-piece every summer and sunbathe in a lawn chair that she would place in the center of her driveway. Every father and son would find outside chores that day to catch a glimpse. She wore her long, thick, wavy blonde hair down and it would bounce with every little movement. Dominique's hair was her best feature—it perfectly framed both eyes on her full face. She also had an older brother named Pat who was just as good looking as her if not better. He was four years older than her, closer to Mack and Edward's age and their friend. Sherry liked Pat. When he would see Sherry in the neighborhood--usually watering his lawn with no shirt--he would say hello and Sherry would giggle. She was too shy to speak to him. Each time, she thought she could say something back, but no words would come out. He was just that fine. Six-feet tall with blonde curly hair, he looked like a surfer and was always tan. Sherry confided in her grandmother about the boys in the neighborhood. Her grandmother would say there must be something in the water for there to be so many gorgeous people and she would tease Sherry by saying, "Pat's so good looking that he literally has you at a loss for words baby?"

The teams played stick it-pick it all day. The first person on one team would swing down the mountain, sitting on a rope knot that was attached high above them on a tree branch. They swung down and stuck the screw driver in the ground, usually in a tight place like between the roots or behind the tree. This was the "stick it" of the game. The opposing team would then have to pick it. They would swing down, only having one chance to grab the screwdriver. Then they would be able to "stick it" for the other team. If they were unsuccessful in the picking, they would earn a letter, working their way up to H-O-R-S-E. Whoever spelled horse first, lost the game.

The boys were showing off and Pete, Vince and Maurice would hang from their feet as they cascaded twenty feet down Everest swinging from a rope. It looked really cool, but obviously dangerous. If you fell you could break your neck. They would wrap one leg in the rope and cross the other leg over it. Hanging upside down allowed your hands to be free and your arms could stretch further in a hanging position. The three became hard to beat because they were able to drive the screwdriver deep into the ground in between the tree trunks. When the other team tried to pick the screwdriver out of the ground it took several tries, which gave them letters quickly.

James Barnes idolized his brother, but this day it was Pete *and* Sherry he was showing off for. The younger Barnes boy decided to go down upside down by his feet too. He pulled the rope swing all the way back and jumped as high as he could to get his leg on the notch. He was determined to pick up the screw driver no one could get. Sherry covered her eyes. *This isn't going to be good,* she thought. She peeped through her fingers. James swung down by his feet at top speed. He was totally out of control. Everyone screamed as they saw him headed straight for a tree. The sound of James' body slamming against the oak tree was sickening. The sound of him hitting the ground came next.

Everyone took off running down the side of the mountain hollering for James. When they reached him, he couldn't move. His back had hit the tree and the impact knocked the wind out of him. While they weren't sure whether the scenario warranted CPR, the kids thought it was better to be safe than sorry. Pete pumped on his chest, trying to remember what he had been taught in Boy Scouts and Vince gave him a few breaths mouth to mouth. James started to cough.

Sherry stood watching with her hand over her mouth. She had a bad feeling all day about something not going right but chalked it up to anxiety about climbing the mountain. There it was; James Barnes almost broke his back. One day she would learn to listen to her intuition, but it was proving to be a tough lesson.

James' accident marked an end to the adventure for that day. They climbed back up the mountain, with the older boys assisting James. Everyone just sat and talked until dusk, trying to make James feel better about being stupid. They told him how cool he looked and how no one else had ever swung that far down. They told him he was lucky to be alive and that there must be something special about him. *That part was true*, thought Sherry. Dominique put her arm around him and kissed him on the cheek. James, being a typical pre-teen felt better and thought it was all worth it after the kiss.

Victor, who always seemed to be in conflict with James, saw a great opportunity to get him back while scoring points with his older brother Vince. Victor jumped on to the rope swing and said, "Hey everybody! Look at me. I'm James!" He pretended to have a long fall off of the swing. Then moaned and groaned like James. Everyone got silent looking at each other for a second to see what sort of reaction would be appropriate. Then everyone busted out in uncontrollable laughter. In typical teenage boy fashion, Victor kept it up for about a half hour. Each time he did the reenactment, Sherry thought it was funnier than the previous time. Sherry laughed so hard her stomach ached. Everyone, including James, was holding their stomachs, with tears rolling down their red faces. For years to come that would be the standard joke whenever they played stick it-pick it.

On the way back home from Everest a few hours later, Bernadette shared with Sherry that some of the gang was planning to stay overnight at the Boy Scout camp. She asked if Sherry would be able to come along

Sherry had not done that kind of a coed overnight before and was sure her father would say no.

"You really think *my* father would allow that?" Sherry said to Bernadette with a doubting look on her face. Bernadette laughed and shook her head. Sherry said goodbye and the girls started to go separate ways when they got to the Sweetstone property.

Before she got far, Bernadette turned back. "Sherry!" she called, running back towards Sherry. "Please tell me you will at least ask to come tonight."

Sherry wasn't looking forward to her father's reaction, but she agreed to ask.

"Well if you come, don't forget to bring an extra flashlight and some snacks. We will have so much fun!"

Sherry could see by the look on Bernadette's face that she already had her hopes up. This got Sherry a little excited too as she began formulating her script, figuring out just what to say to her dad to increase her chances of being allowed on the campout.

As Sherry turned to head towards the house, Maurice caught up with her and said, "I got this. Let me talk to Dad." He had been out camping before and Sherry knew with him going along, she had a better chance.

Maurice waited until Mr. Sweetstone had his dinner and was relaxing. Maurice could see he was in a good mood and seized the moment, asking first if he could go camping.

"Yeah sure. But you be careful up there. Who all is going?"

Maurice named the usual suspects, making sure to name Bernadette too. He nudged Sherry, who was sitting next to him on the couch.

"Dad since Bernadette is coming and her brother is looking out for her, do you think I could go with Maurice this time?" she said, gritting her teeth in anticipation of the response.

Mr. Sweetstone looked over at the two of them, obviously thinking. "I guess I don't see why not."

Sherry couldn't believe it, and from the look on Maurice's face, he was surprised too. Both of them broke out into a little dance, "We're going camping, we're going camping," they chanted. Mr. Sweetstone laughed a little and rolled his eyes at the two of them.

"Go on," he said, shooing them away.

The kids ran up to the attic to find their sleeping bags, and then to pack a bag of snacks and extra equipment.

It was seven in the evening when darkness came upon the path. The moon was full and the light guided Maurice and Sherry. They were to meet up with James, Victor and Bernadette a little ways up the path.

"Who's that?" said James as he heard them approach, intentionally shining his flashlight straight into their eyes.

"Man," said Maurice covering his eyes to block out the glare. "It's your momma James," he joked, getting a laugh out of everyone.

James could be okay sometimes thought Sherry. James took the lead since his older brother Pete wasn't around. He began telling everyone that he brought enough food for them all, from hotdogs to s'mores. He also brought some eggs and sausage for breakfast in the morning. Sherry hadn't realized until now, as she pictured James cooking over an open fire pit, what a grown-up activity camping was. She had camped in her backyard, in a small plastic tent, when she was a little girl. But this was the big leagues.

Sherry thought the path was creepy at night. She wasn't a little kid and would never admit it if anyone asked, but she was a little scared of camping out in the woods, in the dark, with no adults around. As their feet crunched on the leaves below, she couldn't help thinking of the wildlife around here and whether or not she should be worried. As they rounded a bend, the moonlight disappeared behind the thick of the woods and it became very dark. The kids were bumping into one another as they kept their flashlights mostly focused on the ground in front of them. James kept bumping into Sherry, until he finally locked his arm into hers. She let him. She felt better walking with James as she passed by the Whittnore property. Looking into the woods, she could just make out the white paint on the no trespassing signs. Her mind began to wonder as she looked into the woods and imagined shadowy people moving in the darkness. Sherry closed her eyes tight for a moment and thought, *God please don't let my imagination run away with me. They're only trees.* When she opened them, the images were gone. Sherry made a conscious effort not to look up into the woods again until they passed the Whittnore property.

She was glad James had locked arms with her. She didn't care if it led him on; she was frightened by the darkness and was willing to take the risk.

"Here we are," he said, steering Sherry by her arm as they almost passed the opening to the Boy Scout camp.

They crossed onto the bridge, over the creek, and started the hour climb up.

"Hold on," said Maurice, stopping to fill their canteens from the stream.

"I see the Boy Scouts taught you a few things," said Vincent. Both Vincent and James were excellent campers for their age.

The group made their way up to the top and dropped their things. Sherry and Bernadette began to make their way to the wood-built shelter that was designed as a camping lodge. But, they were intercepted by the boys.

"We're not going to sleep under there tonight," said Vincent.

"Why not?" said Bernadette.

"Well," Vincent looked around at the other guys. "It's pretty rocky and you can't see the sky from under there. It's just better to sleep out here in the open," he said, seeming to make things up as he went along.

"What are you even talking about Vincent?" said Bernadette, sensing he wasn't giving them the whole story. "We are too going to sleep in there!"

"Yeah I don't want to be all out in the open," chimed Sherry, not wanting to reveal that her fears were what were driving her into the shelter.

"Look. You don't want to sleep in there. But if you don't believe us, have a look for yourself." James shone his light into the shelter and the girls saw the ground move—wolf spiders scattered everywhere, hiding from the light. Sherry screamed and Bernadette jumped behind her. The boys, on the other hand, laughed crazily. They all knew why you never actually slept in the camping lodge; wolf spiders had made a home of it just months after its completion.

Iceburg

"You're a jerk!" Bernadette said to her brother James.

"Don't yell at me. You wanted to see; shoot you wanted to sleep with them!" James was speaking loudly. He wanted to make certain everyone heard his joke. Yep, thought Sherry, he's back to being himself again, showing off and seeking attention.

Sherry distanced herself from James and looked up into the sky. The moon was shining brightly on the mountain. It was so peaceful. Aside from the kids talking, you could her movement of the birds and night creatures. Fear aside, nighttime in the wilderness was truly beautiful. Bernadette grabbed Sherry's arm. "Come with me into the woods while the guys set up the tents."

Bernadette was not afraid of the woods at night. While they were out going pee, they made a pact that regardless of what time they had to use the bathroom tonight they would accompany each other.

When they returned, they found the boys had set up two tents, a large one for the boys and a smaller one for the girls. They all sat around the huge bonfire James built, roasting hot dogs on sticks. No one knew it but Vincent was working up the nerves to suggest they play spin the bottle. The idea was a little odd considering there were only two girls, their older brothers were around, and one of the girls was black. He didn't care about any of those objections. Tonight he felt he would go against how he was raised and kiss a black girl. The odds of the bottle landing on Bernadette were fifty percent. Being a horny pre-teen he was willing to chance it, secretly hoping it wouldn't land on Sherry, and fortunately it never did.

Vincent didn't believe in interracial anything; that's just how they were raised. But when he moved to River Sades five years ago, everyone seemed to like the Sweetstones and they were nothing like the way his father would describe black people. He was a little apprehensive about getting too close to them at first, and tried to separate James from Maurice. But James wouldn't have it; he and Maurice got to be good friends. As time went on, Vincent realized they were just kids, with no real differences aside from their skin color and hair. Vincent didn't care what his father said. He would never admit it, but occasionally all of that negativity his father had taught him would come through in his thoughts. He would think horrible things about Maurice when they got in disagreements, calling him all sorts of ugly names in his head. But no one knew.

Vincent stood up next to the bonfire ready to suggest his game idea. Before he got a word out, there was a distant howl far-off in the woods. Vincent said with his eyes huge and the fire lighting up his face, "What the hell was that?"

"I don't know," said James as he ran into the tent and came out with his serrated knife. Maurice quickly grabbed a flashlight and shined it into the woods. The three walked toward the edge of Mount Everest and shined the flashlight down the mountain and towards the path leading home. The sound was getting closer and the boys could hear the rustle of something or someone moving quickly on the path towards them.

"Shhh!" said James. "Hear that?" Everyone heard it and he didn't have to ask. Sherry was scared to death. Both girls were on their feet and standing as close together as possible.

"There it is again," Maurice whispered, shining his light on the path, scared at any moment that something wild would come into view. The three boys stood near the top of the path, waiting. They weren't sure what it is they were waiting for but they were as ready as they could be.

"Maybe we should shut off our lights so we don't attract whatever it is," suggested Vincent. All three boys clicked off their flashlights. The girls moved closer to them in the darkness.

"What should we do," said Maurice.

"Kill it," remarked James quickly.

"Don't be stupid James; we don't even know what "it" is yet." Sherry couldn't see Vincent's face but she had a feeling he was looking towards James with disdain.

The girls went back inside their tent and zipped it up, not making a sound. Suddenly the three boys could hear the rustling of leaves down the trail about 50 yards. Something was coming. They heard the howl again and all five got chills. Sitting in the tent, Sherry used the only strategy she knew. "God please let everything be ok." Bernadette would have normally made fun of Sherry for praying, but she was scared too and was glad to hear Sherry looking for a solution. Immediately after her prayer, Sherry felt a sense of peace inside of her. And not a few seconds later, she heard another howl, followed immediately by laughter.

They all knew the laugh; they had been hearing it all day. "Who's there?!" shouted Maurice confidently, turning on his flashlight and shining it down the path. His fear had dissipated and he was perturbed that someone had tricked them, had gotten them all terrified.

The light finally revealed the culprits, a tipsy Dominique Wood and Victor Monkton, stumbling up the path. The two were not alone; they were in the company of a bottle of blackberry brandy and Jack Daniels. At the sound of Victor's voice Bernadette's heart started to beat a mile a minute. She had butterflies in her stomach and felt a sensation in here body that happened whenever Victor was around. She had the hots for Victor and when he gave her the slightest attention, it totally led her on. He knew it and the rumor was that Victor secretly liked younger girls. Of course, he protested that he didn't every chance he got. Bernadette's excitement was tempered by the presence of Dominique's voice. Jealousy would do that. She brushed her hair frantically and emptied her bag upside down, looking for her lip gloss. Sherry had never seen Bernadette lose her cool and her behavior made it obvious just how bad she had it for Victor. Sherry believed Bernadette could hold her own; she was cute. But her little girl looks couldn't hold a candle to Dominique. Bernadette, as beautiful as she was, had one thing working against her and that was her age.

"Who's in there?" Victor said as he poked his head into the tent. He shamelessly almost kissed Bernadette as his face bumped hers when she was getting ready to peep her head out at the same time he put his in. "Well hey there beautiful!" he said, causing her to blush like crazy. She glanced around to see where Dominique was, timing how long she would have his attention. Maurice and James were showing of their camping skills to Dominique. *That could take a while,* she thought.

She made her move quickly. "What are you drinking?"

"It's your favorite," said Victor, smiling big. Bernadette stepped out of the tent and Sherry followed.

"Her favorite? She doesn't even drink," interrupted Sherry.

Bernadette and Victor both laughed. "Yes I do, Sherry. Victor and

I have been drinking blackberry brandy at the beach for the past two months now."

"And she's developed quite a taste for it," Victor added.

Sherry looked back and forth between Bernadette and Victor. She could *feel* the positive tension between them. Bernadette took a drink. "It's good Sherry. Here, try it."

Sherry searched for her brother, noticing he was totally distracted. She grabbed the bottle and made the other two swear to secrecy before taking a quick sip. The brandy was sweet on her tongue for about one second. As she swallowed, the brandy burned her throat and warmed her stomach. Having never tasted alcohol like this before, one sip relaxed her fairly quickly. She felt a little guilty, but shook it off-- it felt like another rite of passage.

Sherry was almost thirteen and told herself that it was an appropriate age to try just a few drinks. She knew her father would kill her if he found out she was drinking; he would never believe that she just tried it once. Knowing him, he would open up an investigation and come to the conclusion that Sherry had been drinking since the age of two. Once Mr. Sweetstone got going, it was impossible to pull back the reigns. She also knew that in order to prove that she wasn't going to snitch on them for drinking liquor at the campout she had better take a drink.

"Let's party!" said a loud voice coming from the edge of the mountain. Sherry turned and looked through the fire and saw the face of Pete Barnes. He had cleaned up well. Sherry began to realize as people kept popping up from the trail onto their campground that this entire night was the brainchild of the older kids, not the younger ones who had gotten here first and set up camp. *How could I have been so naïve?* thought Sherry. She noticed it looked like they had done this before, including Bernadette. Sherry's feelings were a little hurt when she realized Bernadette had been partying with the older crowd and didn't bother to tell her. But she knew she couldn't expect much more since they hardly talked over the summer.

The crowd was getting bigger and bigger. It seemed like most of the kids in town were up on Everest that night. Suddenly Sherry was frightened by the unknown faces. She was very uncomfortable and wanted to go home. She grabbed Bernadette's arm and whispered to her, "Who are these people Bernadette?"

"Relax, Sherry." Bernadette saw the look on her face and knew she needed some reassurance. "Everything's okay. Nothing bad is going to happen. Maurice and Pete are both here and no one is going to mess with you." Bernadette called her oldest brother over and asked him to keep an eye on Sherry. He said no problem, but was soon distracted by all of the girls around. Sherry tried to relax but was clearly way too immature for this crowd.

All the women seemed to know Bernadette and gave her special attention, contributing to Sherry's feeling of isolation. Because of her four good looking brothers, every girl in River Sades kissed Bernadette's butt and called her their little sister, anything to get past the front door. Sherry wondered what other things had gone on over the summer that she didn't know about. She pulled Bernadette aside again and asked her, "So how far have you and Victory gone, Bernadette?"

"I'll tell you later Sherry," she said quickly and took off in Victor's direction. Sherry watched her disappear behind some trees where Victor was waving her to come over. In the distance Sherry could see as they moved back further into the woods, watching until she could their silhouettes disappeared into shadows.

Sherry started to search the crowd for her brother Maurice. She had recognized someone from Desy Cove, and knowing how prejudiced they were in that neighborhood she wanted to give Maurice a heads-up and check on him.

"There you are," said Maurice as he spotted his little sister. She immediately felt better seeing him.

"Hey," she said smiling slightly.

"Whoa sis, you been drinking?"

"I just had a few sips Maurice, just to taste. You aren't going to tell anyone are you?" she asked, already knowing her brother wouldn't betray her like that.

"Nah. Don't worry. Your secret's safe with me."

Sherry still felt completely out of place, but since she couldn't go home, she thought she would seclude herself and try to get to sleep. She knew the faster she fell asleep, the faster morning would arrive. "I'm going to lie down in the tent. Can you make sure I'm safe while I sleep?" said Sherry.

"Yep. Don't worry sis. I'll look out for you. Hey, by the way, did you see Tom Waters was here?" Maurice asked.

"Yeah, I was coming over to make sure you knew some of the Desy Cove kids were here. Will you be okay?"

"Ha! Yes Sherry. I will be fine. I've got plenty of friends here and these fools know better than to try anything."

Sherry made her way back to her tent. As she got inside and turned to zip it closed, she had one last look around. There were kids everywhere. Lanterns were lit and music was playing. She also saw they were smoking. She thought it was cigarettes at first but realized it was pot when she saw the kids passing it around and coughing between fits of wild laughter. She had never been around marijuana before, but she knew that a lot of the older kids smoked it. It only worsened her feelings about the whole campout. She felt guilty by association; she would never camp again unless it was only with the kids her age She didn't feel entirely safe in the tent but she didn't feel so self-conscious and out of place, so it would have to do.

Bernadette melted as Victor kissed her long and hard. He put his hands up and down her young body and she wanted more. She had let him feel her up before but she hoped he would finally go further. She was nervous but felt ready. They were out in the woods and he had laid out a blanket for her. He touched her all over with the gentlest of hands. The first time they had made out, Bernadette couldn't believe how gentle he was. She didn't realize that a man (and she considered Victor more man than boy) could touch so softly and with such care. Victor took his time with Bernadette; he did not want to scare her off. She surprised him by initiating more every time they were together. They were only four years apart, but some people would say she was way too young for him. Bernadette knew that when adults got into relationships, sometimes decades separated them, so this didn't feel like anything immoral at all, at least no more immoral than making out with someone your own age.

Victor spoke softly to Bernadette, "Are you ready to go all the way?"

"MmmHmm," Bernadette moaned her approval. Knowing it was her first time, he wanted to make it special for her. That night would be forever etched in her memory and he knew it. Unfortunately, what Bernadette didn't know is that she would fight to live down a reputation after that night, after losing her virginity at such a young age to such a known ladies-man.

Chapter 5
Making Good on a Promise

While heading up the driveway, alongside Larence and her dogs, Sherry remembered tomorrow was laundry day and she had to get her coat in the wash. The sleeves smelled of smoke from every now and again taking a drag off Kara's cigarette. Sherry promised her mom she wouldn't smoke again since the time she and Kara were caught by Ty Bateman. He snuck into Kara's backyard one day trying to catch a glimpse of them in their bathing suits. He was always being a peeping tom. This hot summer day he caught them smoking.

"Ooh! I'm gonna tell," said Ty. Kara and Sherry begged him not to, as if there life depended on it. He tried blackmail.

"Let me use your canoe for a month," he directed his bribe towards Kara.

"No way. You can have it for a week."

He agreed and promised not to say a word. Sherry knew in her gut not to trust Ty. He was a snake. This is why they never hung out with him, despite him only being a year younger and living nearby. He would hold things over their heads and loved nothing more than to get other people in trouble. On many days he would take out Kara's sail boat, not the canoe as bargained. For weeks this went on, Ty would come by uninvited. Sherry and Kara would hide when he knocked on Kara's front door. He would wait around for hours, messing around outside and just sitting on the porch, as if he knew they were hiding inside. Sherry and Kara agreed

Iceburg

that they had both had enough of Ty. He was becoming a pain in the ass. They needed to find a way to get rid of him, something that would get *him* in trouble. But that meant they would have to follow him around to get some dirt on him. While the plan was tempting, they both decided that was not a good idea. Following through would make them no better than him. And they were really not interested in being around him anymore than absolutely necessary.

Ty spoke to Sherry's father from time to time. He was a real brown-noser and knew Mr. Sweetstone was a very strict man. One day, Ty showed up at Kara's house and wanted to swim at Kara's private beach-front. Kara, of course, said no. In response, he threatened to tell on Kara for smoking, and Sherry too simply for being around, though he didn't see her actually take a drag. Ty stormed off of Kara's property.

"I'm not worried about ole Ty Bateman. He is full of hot air," Kara said to Sherry. But despite his often-made empty threats, something felt different to Sherry this time.

"I don't know Kara, he sounds serious this time."

Kara knew she wouldn't have any consequences if Ty told her mother she had been smoking. Kara's mother couldn't have care less what Kara was up to. Everyone, including Ty, knew that. Ty knew he would get more mileage out of this information if he told on Sherry. He knew Mr. Sweetstone would be mad and Sherry would get punished. Ty figured she would be grounded and wouldn't be able to spend time with Kara. In one way or another, Kara would feel his wrath. *Two for the price of one*, thought Ty.

"I believe he might actually make good on his threat today," Sherry said. "C'mon, let's go."

The girls took off after Ty, following him down Rogers Hill and headed in between houses. He cut around some houses and they lost track of him for a minute. Sherry thought maybe she had been wrong and that he was really headed home. But, he popped out at the end of River Sades and was headed towards Sherry's house.

"That rat!" screamed Kara. Sherry and Kara picked up their pace. Sherry knew her mom was home and really didn't know how she would respond. They couldn't catch him in time. By the time they reached the end of Sherry's driveway, Ty was knocking on her front door.

"Who is it?" she called out as she walked towards the door. She saw Ty through the screen door and motioned him to come onto the porch. "Hey Ty. How are you?"

Mrs. Sweetstone was well aware of Ty's sneaky ways and wondered what he was doing. None of her children played with him so she assumed he was here to brown nose with Mr. Sweetstone. Sherry and Kara ducked behind a tree, knowing it was too late to intervene and deciding to hide, watch and wait. Ty began to explain how he caught the girls smoking and felt it was his duty to tell an adult. He wasn't there long, before Sherry's mom saw right through him.

"Thanks for coming and telling me Ty." She told him that she would handle things and that it wasn't worth bothering Mr. Sweetstone about. As he turned to leave, the girls saw the smug look on his face and Sherry became sick to her stomach. Sherry and Kara contemplated weather or not to go into Sherry house now or later. They both choose to get it over with. Kara liked Sherry's mom and Sherry's mother thought Kara was one of the nicer girls in River Sades. They both went into Sherry's house. Mrs. Sweetstone met them at the door with a disappointed look on her face. Surprisingly, though, she didn't seem angry.

"You better be happy that I was the one he told and not your father. Pray he don't find out!" she told them with a serious look on her face.

Mrs. Sweetstone was right; the outcome would have been far different if it was Mr. Sweetstone that had spoken to Ty. The house would be in an uproar for days and Sherry may have been grounded indefinitely. The thought of that not happening, ironically, put her in a good mood despite the fact that her mother had just found out she was smoking. But before she had a chance to crack a smile, Mrs. Sweetstone sat the girls down right away and talked to them about smoking, what a nasty habit it was, and how it could make you look like an old lady way before your time.

"Sherry I can stop you from smoking now, but what you do when you're 18 is your business. As long as you live under our roof though, you are to do as you're told and I'm telling you right now that I don't want you smoking. If I find out you are doing it again, I won't save you from your daddy." The lecture went on, but Sherry zoned out after she understood the gist of it.

"Now get out of here," her mother concluded, and the girls began to walk away with their heads hung low. But Kara couldn't resist the opportunity to bad mouth Ty and explain herself.

"Mrs. Sweetstone," she started off in the sweetest tone she could muster. "Ty had caught us smoking and has been holding it over our heads for weeks threatening us the whole time."

"I got the feeling he was up to something. Listen," she said, turning to Sherry. "I don't want that boy comin' around here, no more you hear me?"

"Yes ma'am," said Sherry gladly. She apologized to her mother and said she wouldn't smoke.

The pressure from Kara and trying to fit in soon caused her to break that promise to her mother. But, she figured, that was just something that kids did as they grew up."

Chapter 6

Iceburg

Sherry quickly navigated her feet up the icy graveled driveway to the house. She had just got off the bus and was ready to get to Kara's house. Kara called Sherry every day after school, to get together. She also called to see what Sherry was wearing to school the next day so she could have Sherry bring her something to wear. Putting on Sherry's clothes made Kara feel thinner. Kara Lemon could not fit Sherry's clothes. But it seemed to Sherry that she wore everything three sizes too small anyways. It didn't matter whether she was wearing her own or Sherry's, her belly would hang out. They had opposite physiques—Sherry was slim and athletic and Kara was on the heavy side. Sherry didn't want to hurt Kara's feelings though, so she would let her borrow the biggest of her clothes and say no to the ones Kara would definitely stretch-out. Sherry had four brothers. Her family was not as rich as Kara's. Therefore her parents could not afford Sherry's close to get ruined.

Kara lived on the Severn River in River Sades, and although it was just across the road from Sherry's house, you had to have a little more money to buy a house within the confines of that community. The Sweetstones were as big of a part of the community as you could be, from the outside. Going to the same school and hanging with all the kids from River Sades made them sort-of honorary members.

Kara had just received a new pair of ice skates for her birthday. As Sherry changed into her outdoor clothes to hang out with Kara, she kept thinking about those skates. *I know she's going to want me to go on the ice with her.* The thought of getting out on the ice made her stomach sick. She knew something bad was going to happen to Larence. She remembered again the dream of her younger brother falling through the ice. It had been a few years ago now, but she had woke up to her heart racing.

As Sherry got older and these dreams became more and more common, she was learning to trust them, hoping that she would eventually not be caught off guard when they did come to fruition. Though she didn't understand what was happening, she knew in her heart God was doing something with her, that this was some sort of gift. She just had to figure out how to use it. So every night she would look up at her ceiling fan while lying in bed, praying and talking to God. She had hoped for a better life. While there was a lot of love in her home, there was also a lot of strain and tension. Her father's drinking had gotten progressively worse and they never knew if he was going to let the rage that sometimes came with it overcome him. Sherry knew her brothers were scared, and though her mother put on a brave face, she sensed that even her resolve was being tested. Being over Kara's almost every day gave her an outlet.

The phone rang. Sherry had butterflies in here stomach, sensing Kara would pressure her to get out on the ice today. She wanted to tell her best friend so bad, about her secret, about her gift. After all, her mother always said, "Tell a dream it won't come true." It was Kara on the phone.

"Hey," she said to Sherry. "So, can you come up?"

"Yeah, I'll be ready in ten minutes. Will you meet me half way?" asked Sherry.

"Sure. I'll see you in ten," said Kara before hanging up. They never required more than a few moments on the phone, unless of course the weather was bad and Kara was in the mood to gossip.

Halfway between the girls was Rodgers Hill. Sherry recollected the time when Kara taught her how to really roller skate. It was a year ago, the day after Christmas. Sherry had received a pair of roller skates the day before, the kind you fit your shoes in. After Sherry practiced on her street for weeks, she was confident enough to skate around the kids in River Sades. Sherry felt proud she taught herself how to roller skate. One day she took her skates to Kara's house. They skated for hours around her block and back and forth in front of her house. Kara was an excellent skater, though she wasn't very athletic. Roller and ice skating were definitely her sports. Kara taught Sherry some moves like figure eights and crossovers. They even skated backwards. Sherry was feeling pretty good about herself. Kara thought for sure she could convince Sherry to skate down the hill with her. But when she suggested it, Sherry's heart dropped. She was feeling good, but was still relatively green and not confident that she could handle that kind of speed. Any other time she had worn her skates and needed to descend a hill like that, she walked along the side of the hill in the dirt while Kara sped down.

"I'll go first," Kara said as they both stood atop the hill. And before Sherry had a chance to tell her that she wouldn't be following, Kara was gone. Dust was flying up from her wheels and her hair was flying out back behind her. She reached the bottom and skid sideways to stop. She turned with a giant grin on her face.

"Sherry come down!" she had screamed from the bottom of the hill. "I'll catch you!"

Sherry shook her head left and right. "No way!" She began to walk over to the side so she could descend in the grass.

"Wait Sherry. Please," said Kara with her most convincing and dependable best friend voice. "I promise, I won't let you get hurt."

Sherry stood staring down at Kara, who seemed so far away. She swore the hill was bigger now than it had ever been. Sherry knew that she was more athletic than Kara. While Kara may be a better skater overall, she thought, I can pick up on things quickly. This shouldn't be too hard.

"You promise you'll help me stop?" she hollered down to Kara.

"I promise. C'mon!"

Sherry trusted her friend. Kara had deceived her before and she wasn't sure why she still trusted her, but, Kara was one of a very select few people she trusted outside of her family. With that thought, she swallowed the butterflies that were creeping out of her stomach and into her throat, and took a step over the edge of the hill.

Sherry was flying down the hill; the bottom of the hill was coming faster than she anticipated. As she neared Kara, she prepared for Kara to put out her arms and reach for her, reaching her own out in anticipation.

Iceburg

But Kara didn't. She stepped to the side and smiled as Sherry came flying past. She turned to watch her go by without saying a word or making any attempt to help her stop. Picking up speed and going over the next much smaller hill, Sherry was frightened. *That bitch!* She knew she couldn't fall now. She had to show Kara. The speed from the hill took Sherry all through the entire neighborhood. She dogged cars and a few kids playing in the street. Finally she began to slow down. It wasn't until she stopped that she cautiously turned around, knees still shaking from the ride.

She turned and saw Kara far behind her laughing. Sherry fully expected to be furious. But once her heart rate subsided a little and she realized the adrenaline rush flooding over her, all she could do was laugh too. She laughed as she skated towards Kara. But that didn't mean she forgave Kara's actions. Sherry was crushed by Kara's deceit. Sherry was used to seeing Kara treat other folks this way, but she thought she was the exception. Sherry finally got her turn. She had been warned by others but had ignored them when it came to Kara. Now she knew that her friendship didn't exclude her from Kara's lack of respect. From that day forward Sherry watched her back when it came to Kara.

On her way to meet up with Kara, walking along the street of River Sades, Sherry knew the names of all the families living in each house. Ms. Rodgers' house was about midway through the neighborhood. Her home was at the base of Rodgers Hill and the reason the hill got its name. Ms. Carol Rodgers was a God-fearing woman who had become a single mom after a bitter divorce. Such things were not the norm in the early seventies. She was an average looking woman, very petite, with red hair and pale skin. She didn't stand out in the crowd, at least not anymore. She had an outer beauty, but it had been doused by the man who was formerly her husband. Now, all that was left was the inner beauty and that too was fading. Most of the time, Carol looked worn out.

Sherry occasionally babysat for Carol and smiled as she thought about her babysitting jobs, grateful that she still had them. Kara wasn't so lucky. She had lost her only babysitting job after one night and now no River Sades' mothers would hire her. It was another point of contention between the girls. The moms of River Sades loved Sherry and Bernadette, who dominated the business. Sherry looked at Ms. Rodgers home and remembered back on all the nights she babysat there. It was a retreat from her own home. She was able to get out of the house and be at peace watching whatever she wanted on TV and eating snacks her mother never kept in the house. For a few months, Sherry didn't even tell Kara that she was sitting for Ms. Rodgers. She was only ten when she got the job and was very responsible and mature; she had to be as one of Carol's two children was a baby. One night she was watching the kids, the phone rang. It happened to be Kara on the other end. Sherry wasn't sure how she had found her there.

"How come you didn't tell me you were sitting for Ms. Rodgers?" said Kara in an accusing tone.

"Because I'm not allowed to have people over, so I figured I would just not mention it," Sherry said hoping it would stop Kara from asking what she knew was on her mind.

"C'mon Sherry, let me come over for a little while. I'm bored and she'll never know."

Sherry had known this would happen if Kara found out. "Kara, I can't. The older kid would tell her mom and I need this job."

Sherry knew if she asked Ms. Rodgers ahead of time she could have a friend over, but she never asked because she didn't want anyone over; she didn't want anyone ruining her little getaway. But Sherry was easily convinced and buckled under pressure. "Listen Kara, you can come over this one time. But that's it. You can't stay long and you have to wait until the kids are asleep."

"Cool," said Kara "I have a surprise for you." Before Sherry could respond, Kara had hung up the phone.

Sherry was nervous the rest of the night. She knew Kara could easily get her in trouble and wasn't really keen on this "surprise" that she mentioned. She thought about locking all the doors, closing the blinds and shutting down the lights. But she knew Kara was just the type to ring the bell until she opened the door. Sherry was preoccupied most of the evening, anticipating how things would go. She couldn't believe she agreed to let her come over, going against her better judgment when it came to Kara. And

Iceburg

Kara knew that Sherry was a pushover at times, that all she had to do was beg a little to get her way. It was true, Sherry had a tough time saying no, especially to the people she valued. And despite all the wrong that Kara had done, she still had a place in Sherry's life. That paired with the fact that Sherry was a little scared of Kara, she kept her around. The two had many secrets together and Sherry always worried when they got into an argument or a falling out that Kara would let those secrets out. Kara knew it too. She was a master manipulator and took Sherry's kindness for weakness at every opportunity. In all honesty, Sherry would have been better off letting her tell it all. At least then she would be free and not held hostage by a dysfunctional friend. Sherry was very forgiving when it came to Kara she thought she needed her as a friend. They been through so much together that Sherry compromised her own better judgment and overlooked many things she didn't agree with to keep the friendship.

A tap came to the downstairs sliding glass doors. Sherry's heart dropped a little as she saw Kara and Vincent at the door. In some ways Sherry was a little relieved when she saw him though. In an effort to impress Vincent, Kara would likely be on her best behavior. Whenever there was a boy around, Kara tried to be an angel. This despite everyone in the neighborhood knowing she wasn't. Sherry stepped outside, setting the ground rules for company right away.

"You all can't come in. I can hang out here for an hour and then you need to go. Ms. Rodgers will be home soon," she said matter-of-factly.

The ground was covered with a light snow and the three made their way to the kids' jungle gym to have a seat. Vincent pulled out a joint and lit it. He passed it to Kara. Sherry stayed silent as it became clear why Kara came. She would love nothing more than to ruin Sherry's babysitting job. She was jealous and spiteful, but Sherry wasn't about to let her get a rise out of her. *They can do what they want. I don't even care,* Sherry thought. Kara noticed the look on Sherry face--she could read Sherry like a book.

"What's the matter? Are you mad at us? Are you going to tell on us?"

That thought hadn't crossed her mind, but maybe she would tell. At that point she was ready to have Kara out of her life.

"No," said Sherry flatly. "What are you guys getting into later?"

Victor was smart and caught on to what Kara was trying to do, feeling

Sherry out about her loyalty. They whispered to each other and Sherry began to feel uncomfortable.

"Look, I'm going in if you two are going to talk among yourselves," said Sherry.

"Wait!" said Kara. "Do you want to try this?" The look on their faces was real crazy almost cunning. They weren't going to let her get out of it. She knew what they were doing. Sherry couldn't get them in trouble if she was smoking too. A chill raced down her back as she reluctantly reached out and grabbed the joint. She put it to her mouth and took a small puff. It definitely tasted different than a cigarette and she began hacking uncontrollably immediately after exhaling. Vincent and Kara were laughing at her.

"Go ahead," said Vincent. "Take another one."

Sherry did until a calm and mellow, yet paranoid feeling came over her. It seemed like everything was cool and no one had a care in the world as the three laughed and joked in the night. Sherry was sitting at the top of the slide and the other two were on the swings. She suddenly remembered she was supposed to be babysitting.

"Oh shit!" said Sherry. "What time is it? I need to get inside." The slide on the jungle gym was still icy from the freezing rain and snow. Trying to be cool, Sherry stood at the top of the slide and attempted to run down it. She made it to the bottom, but her old sneakers had no tread and her right foot slipped from underneath her. She went flying into the air. Time stood still for a moment as she was airborne. Hoping her head wouldn't hit the metal slide; she looked at all the stars and knew she had made a huge mistake when she allowed Kara to come over. Her life flashed in front of her. *God please help me* she thought just before she landed. Her butt hit the ground and the base of her skull hit the edge of the slide. Sherry lay there for what seemed like an eternity, listening to the two stoners laugh. They thought she was playing.

"Help me," whimpered Sherry. She stared at the stars and wasn't quite sure what hurt, or if she could feel anything at all. Vincent came into her line of sight and kneeled down next to her.

"Shut up Kara! I think she's really hurt."

Soon Kara was kneeling on the other side of her. "Are you okay?"

Iceburg

"No," was all Sherry could manage. She couldn't verbalize how she felt because it was hard to talk and because she still wasn't sure what to say. She started to panic.

"Kara, help me sit her up," said Vincent, doing the worst possible thing you could to someone with a potential neck or head injury.

They lifted her to a sitting position and talked to her calmly. Vincent looked at the back of her head, touching gently. He gasped at the knot that had formed so quickly.

"I think you have a concussion Sherry. We need to get you up and moving around."

Sherry wasn't sure where Vincent had gotten his medical training or where he had heard that moving around is good for a concussion. But, she wasn't in a position to ask questions and instead simply did as she was told. They each took one side of Sherry, lifting gently under her arms and wrapping them over their own shoulders.

"How does that feel?" asked Vincent.

"Okay, I guess," responded Sherry, still dazed. "I think I need to lie down though." She felt incredibly sleepy.

"Let's get her inside," suggested Kara.

"You can't let anyone with a concussion fall asleep," Vincent said, raising his voice and obviously panicked about Sherry.

"Listen, I'm fine. Just let me go in and get something to drink. You guys need to leave anyways. I'll be okay." Sherry's head was beginning to clear up a little and she knew she had to get the two of them out of there before Ms. Rodgers got home.

Kara began brushing the dirt and snow off of Sherry's clothes. Sherry was a little taken aback by her friend's caring touch. They helped her inside and sat her on the couch.

"Listen Sherry," said Vincent standing over her. "You can't fall asleep." Sherry found his fatherly tone a little humorous, but she knew he was right. "If you get sleepy, you need to stand up and walk around, okay?"

"Yeah. Okay. Now get out of here."

The two began to leave and Kara looked back at Sherry, "Call me when you get home," she said with a genuine look of concern in her eyes.

After they had left, Sherry went to the fridge and got a Coke. She thought she would go upstairs and check on the kids as soon as she rested a little. She sat down on the sofa, and turned on the TV. She put her feet up and rested her head. She knew she wasn't supposed to fall asleep but thought if she could just relax for a little while she would feel better. What if she did have a concussion? She wondered if she should call for help, or if she should have let Kara stay behind to keep an eye on her. But she knew she would have a hard time explaining the situation to Ms. Rodgers. She thought about the kids, and that they probably needed to be looked in on. She was so tired though. She would just rest a moment, and then check on the kids. Ms. Rodgers could always take her to the hospital if she felt worse when she arrived home. All of these thoughts were swimming through her cloudy head, but she couldn't focus or concentrate. Finally, she gave into the sleepiness and drifted off.

The clock clanged and startled Sherry awake. It took her a moment to remember where she was, looking at her surroundings to get her bearings. She slowly sat upon the sofa and the pounding in her head reminded her of what had happened earlier in the evening. She got to her feet, taking inventory of how she felt. Her mind was definitely clearer than it had been before; now she just had a headache. She looked at the clock and realized it was 2 a.m. She must have dozed off and slept for a good hour. Ms. Rodgers would be home any minute. She decided to peek in on the kids, who were sleeping soundly. Sherry took a moment to thank God for her health. She thought about what Vincent had said, that she might not wake up if she allowed herself to fall asleep, and she was grateful despite the pounding in her skull.

Sherry had some clarity now and was no longer feeling the effects of the pot. She knew she had made several mistakes that evening, first in allowing Kara to come over and secondly in smoking weed out of peer pressure. They had talked about peer pressure at school and Sherry always laughed it off. But it happened just how the teachers warned them, and she realized then how hard it could be to say no to friends.

Sherry straightened up the house, putting away toys and throwing away the remnants of an earlier snack just as Ms. Rodgers' car pulled in the driveway. Sherry decided it was best if she didn't say anything about the accident and her injury. She was feeling better and didn't want to run the risk of losing Ms. Rodgers' trust or her babysitting job.

Later Sherry would be warned by Ms. Rodgers specifically that Kara couldn't come over. She knew the girls were friends and didn't want Kara around the kids, especially after she had been spotted by her daughter Lucy kissing Richard Rondowski in the living room after she had been put to bed. Kara didn't understand it was a privilege to watch someone's child. Sherry guessed this was because Kara's own mother didn't take her role as a parent very seriously. Kara didn't have the best example on how to act around children. After Kara had gotten fired by Ms. Rodgers, and her mother discovered the ladies in River Sades were hiring Sherry instead, she called around in a drunken rant, asking the women why they would choose Sherry, who didn't even technically live in the community, over her daughter. What she really meant to ask was why you would hire a little black girl over Kara.

Staring at the Rodgers house, Sherry also recalled the time, just a few months back, when she needed to talk to an adult about what was going on in her 12-year old world. She needed direction and guidance and felt she didn't always get that at home. Some things, Sherry knew, were too big for her to handle, like her dreams. The problem was, she didn't feel safe sharing these things with anyone older, more equipped. So she gave up on talking about it and kept it all inside, choosing instead to keep those things between God and herself.

"Remember the time you asked me if I believe in God?" Sherry asked Ms. Rodgers one day after ending a babysitting session.

"Of course."

"Well do you think I could go to church with you this Sunday?"

"Absolutely, I'll pick you up on my way, at around 10," Ms. Rodgers said, wondering why Sherry had the change of heart. When she had asked her about her faith close to a year ago, Sherry seemed to get very uncomfortable, so she dropped the issue and decided to let it go.

At church that Sunday, Sherry went through the motions. But, Ms. Rodgers senses that she had something on her mind. In an effort to crack the shell she sensed Sherry was hiding behind, she invited her over for brunch after service.

"So," said Ms. Rodgers as she assembled some sandwiches. "What is going on with you?"

Sherry felt like she was under interrogation. She took a big gulp of lemonade to buy her some time. She didn't know where to begin and it was so rare that an adult actually seemed interested in what was going through her head that she struggled to find the right words. She took a deep breath and just said it.

"I dream the future."

Immediately after she blurted it out, she was embarrassed. It sounded stupid, she was convinced. She felt her face flush and her eyes fill with tears. Ms. Rodgers would probably think she was crazy, or making it up, or both. She quickly amended her statement.

"Well, I think I dream the future. Sometimes I have dreams and they come true later. It's happened a lot and is happening more and more. But, no one really knows except my family who doesn't believe me." The string of words just kept tumbling from her mouth.

"There is just so much fighting in my house between my folks that I can barely concentrate in school and lately I've been getting these massive migraine headaches."

"Do you have one now?" said Ms. Rodgers calmly.

"No," said Sherry. "It usually only happens in my last class as I get ready to go home. When I told my mom about the headaches she didn't believe me; she thought I was seeking attention. She doesn't deal well with problems. I guess she is just busy working, trying to put food on the table. So she gets around to taking me seriously whenever she can."

Ms. Rodgers had sat down across from Sherry and listened quietly. *This poor girl has just been waiting for someone to* listen, she thought.

"I had to beg her for medicine and she didn't get it for me until I offered to use my babysitting money. She used to give me some of her aspirin but that didn't do anything but make me sick to my stomach. I don't like her Ms. Rodgers. She is mean to me; she makes me go to work with her and calls me names." Sherry wasn't sure what made her share the last few details. Her mouth was a leaking faucet and everything she had held back was pouring forth.

"Do your parents hit you?" Ms. Rodgers asked, worried about Sherry's wellbeing.

"No. I've gotten a spanking before but it was a long time ago." Sherry didn't want to get her parents in trouble and realized that Ms. Rodgers would call the police if she thought Sherry was in danger. She chose her words carefully. Her parents weren't physically abusive, but the house was definitely not a calm, safe place.

"My dad drinks a lot and has a bad temper, but he wouldn't beat me." Sherry thought about the times she had seen her dad in a drunken rampage, taking it out on the boys. But for Sherry, his drinking merely meant harsh words and cold stares.

"Look Sherry. I know you aren't used to talking like this and I can tell you are nervous. You can trust me. I won't say a word."

Sherry looked at Ms. Rodgers and saw in her eyes that she was sincere. Maybe it was because they had gone to church together or because Ms. Rodgers trusted Sherry with her kids. But Sherry knew she had found a confidant.

"No they don't beat me; they just make me feel bad. They call me names and tell all of us how much easier life would be without 'so many mouths to feed.'" Sherry said the last part with serious sarcasm in her voice.

"You know Sherry, I asked Mr. Rodgers to leave some time ago because of his issues with alcohol." Ms. Rodgers was opening up to Sherry, giving her something to relate to. And in just those few words, Sherry was comforted. She knew she couldn't be the only one going through stuff like this and it helped to know that even adults struggled with similar problems. She let out a huge sigh of relief.

Finally, thought Sherry, *someone believes me.* Then her eyes welled up and she began to sob uncontrollably. Ms. Rodgers put her arms around Sherry and comforted her.

"Anytime you need to talk Sherry, I'm here." She went on to tell Sherry that her dreams were obviously a gift, something special God gave her to set her apart from other kids. She just needed to trust him. And then she said something that Sherry would never forget.

"God doesn't give us anything we can't handle. You might not know why you are going through these things now or how to use your gift, but he'll make it clear to you at the right time."

Ms. Rodgers felt blessed that she could be a role model to Sherry. Having been through some of the same things, she felt like she was put in Sherry's life at this point for a reason, to guide her and be a source of support.

"Look Sherry," she went on with a serious look on her face. "You don't have to like how your parents act. When the Bible says, 'Honor thy father and mother,' it's assuming your father and mother are acting in accordance with the ways of God. Your parents have an obligation to do the right thing too. The way they treat you isn't right, and I know it can be hard for you to deal with."

You don't know the half, thought Sherry.

"I'll be praying for you and you do the same. Know that those things that your parents say to you when they are upset are not true. You are valuable and you are valued. Don't get your sense of self-esteem from someone who isn't following God's way. Get your confidence from knowing that God has your back and he wouldn't have given you your gift if he didn't think you were a very special person."

Ms. Rodgers may have been super-Christian, but she did know exactly what to say. She left Sherry feeling completely validated and relieved that day. She wasn't sure if reading the Bible would help, like Ms. Rodgers suggested, but she knew that her discussions with God made her feel better on a daily basis, and that Ms. Rodgers interpretation of things just felt right.

Kara's cheeks were red and stood out on her pale face. Sherry laughed to herself. Kara couldn't even catch a tan in August. She came over the hill all bundled up. It was the coldest day in February. The look on her face was full of excitement.

"Hey! What do you want to get into today?"

Iceburg

Anything but smoking and skating, thought Sherry. "Let's go to your house, and arrange the dolls."

They both knew they were too old for it. But playing with dolls brought them both comfort. Something about making a perfect household with perfect miniature people gave them hope for their own little lives. And with all of the dolls and accessories that Kara had, it was easy to make a perfect home. Her parents had forgotten about love and nurturing, instead choosing to comfort Kara with things.

"Oh come on," said Kara. "I'm tired of being inside. Let's do something different."

"Kara I'm freezing! Can we at least go warm up for a little bit?"

The girls finished the walk to Kara's house, where they made hot chocolate and ate cookies. While Sherry was standing in the kitchen looking out the window, Kara stepped outside to smoke. At thirteen, Kara must have thought she had reached the age where she didn't have to hide her rebellion from her mother. In all honesty, with her mom's level of commitment to her, she probably could have started smoking at home much sooner and still not gotten in trouble.

Sherry could see the cottages across the frozen river. Kara's house had a great view and Sherry wondered if her and her mother would continue to live in the hulking place after her parents' divorce was finalized. Kara came back inside, slamming the sliding door shut.

"Looks like the older kids made it across the river," said Kara. "The river must be frozen solid."

Oh no-- here it comes, thought Sherry.

Kara turned to Sherry. "How about we just hang out on the beach in the snow? You can stay ashore, while I tryout my new skates by the pier."

"Okay," Sherry said, wondering if Kara was up to something or if it was okay to be relieved that Kara was respecting her wishes to not get on the ice. "But don't ask me to go out on the ice," she said just in case.

"I know; I know." said Kara.

Kara was a frequent liar and Sherry knew better than to trust her. It seemed like every time they were together, Sherry was questioning their friendship. It wasn't that Sherry continued to trust her, she knew better.

It was that she took friendship and loyalty very seriously, no matter how lightly Kara took it

Kara was a skilled ice skater. She did figure eights and fancy moves while Sherry watched from the snow-covered beach. Looking across the Severn River, Sherry could see no one was on it. There were a few kids in the distance, skating on the Magothy, but even they seemed to be keeping close to the shore. Neither river was that far across, but in the rainy months the flows could get treacherous and no one could be sure how deep the water was.

Kara came skating closer. "Okay Sherry. What gives? Why don't you want to get out here with me?"

Sherry was always reluctant to talk about her dreams. Despite her discussion with Ms. Rodgers, she was worried they would make her seem like some kind of freak. She knew Kara was a rat and she couldn't trust her, but she also knew that telling her the truth might get her off of her back.

"I had a dream that Larence fell through the ice," she said plainly.

"Oh wow," said Kara. "Well that makes sense, but you don't have to worry. Larence isn't out here and the ice is thick."

Sherry knew Kara wouldn't be able to just let her be on the bank without pressuring her to get on the ice. She looked up at the sky. It was a gorgeous day, despite the cold. The clouds in the distance were a light purple and the bright sun cast yellows on their edges. Sherry always loved the way the sky looked after a winter snow storm. *Please God, let everything be okay today.* Sherry knew that Kara was right, that Larence wasn't out here. She tried telling herself that her fear was irrational. After all, she hadn't dreamt that *she* would be the one to fall through the ice.

"Come on Kara, let's skate, "said Sherry. Sherry didn't have skates with her. Actually, she didn't own a pair of skates. But on this ice, you didn't really need blades and Sherry's old, treadles sneakers slid around just fine. It was fun to slide around and Sherry chose to focus on that rather than the growing sense of dread in her stomach.

In the distance, someone was skating towards them.

"Who's that?" shouted Kara.

"It kinda looks like Bernadette," said Sherry as she squinted in the bright sun.

Iceburg

"Grrrrreat," Kara drew out the word to express her lack of excitement. Not only was Bernadette beautiful, but she skated more gracefully than Kara simply because she was a smaller size.

"Hi," said Bernadette as she skated closer. "I'm sooo glad to see you guys," she said. "The older gang's across the river and I'm stuck here with the younger kids. Do you all want to skate with me across the river?"

Kara spoke up quickly, "Sure!"

"Who's all by the beach?" asked Sherry.

"I don't know," said Bernadette. "A bunch of littler kids. Your brother Larence is over there. They are playing Iceberg."

Sherry froze and immediately flashed back to her dream. She was sick to her stomach as she turned to look at Kara, who had gone pale.

"I've got to get over there and check on him. Kara, are you coming?"

Before Kara could answer, Bernadette interrupted, speaking to Kara, "Guess who's across the river."

"Who?" said Kara, answering Bernadette and ignoring her "best friend" Sherry for the moment.

"Richard Rondowski," said Bernadette, knowing that Kara had a crush on him. Bernadette seemed to use any opportunity she had to prove to Sherry what a shallow friend Kara really was.

Bernadette had it in for Kara ever since she had her over for a sleepover and Kara had gotten into Mrs. Barnes liquor cabinet. When her mother discovered that some of her booze was missing, Bernadette begged Kara to come clean. Kara denied it up until James, Bernadette's older brother, found the missing bottles in her overnight bag. From that day, Kara wasn't allowed at the Barnes' house.

Richard loved the ladies and the ladies loved him. He was very suave and mature for his age all off sixteen, six-feet tall with dark brown thick hair and huge brown eyes to match his tan face. Richard was very hairy for his age, which was a definite topic for teasing from the other guys, attraction from the older girls, and uncertainty from the young ones. Richard and Kara lived next door to one another. Truly, he had no love interest in Kara. But she made it easy for him and they really were good friends, having grown up so close together. Richard and Kara shared their home life secrets and it wasn't pretty. There was camaraderie in their pain.

To Richard, Kara could not be his girl. But he was a typical sixteen year old male, meaning if he could feel her up, he would. Kara mistook the make out sessions for love. Kara had mistaken lot of things. Richard was the boy Kara had lost her one and only babysitting job over.

Kara's bad intentions

Ms. Rodgers, being a godly woman, felt sorry for Kara having a drunk for a mom and thought maybe babysitting could give her some balance and esteem. On her way to babysit that evening, Richard yelled out his window to Kara as she walked away from her house.

"Where are you going?" he hollered.

"Going to babysit the Rodgers' kids," she replied, holding her head high. She thought it might get some points with Richard, that maybe he would think she was worthy of motherhood. Maybe it would make her more attractive.

"Want some company?" he yelled back.

"I'll call you later Richard," she said flatly, doing her best to seem uninterested.

When Ms. Rodgers met Kara she didn't have a warm fuzzy feeling about her but she felt she would be responsible enough to watch her children for a few hours. After all, the neighbors kept a good eye on the house when she went to choir practice. *How much can happen in a few hours?* thought Ms. Rodgers. Kara played briefly with Lucy the six year old and held the infant for a while. She fed them, changed a diaper and put them to bed. Though a part of her melted at Joseph's innocence when she held him, her awe was short-lived.

As soon as she had got the kids to bed, she called Richard and invited him over.

"Come to the basement sliding door," said Kara. "And don't knock—I'll just be waiting for you."

In ten minutes Richard's face appeared at the glass door. Kara slid the door back and stepped out. Putting her hand over Richard's mouth as he was about to speak.

"Shh! The kids are sleeping."

"Okay!" he whispered loudly. "So, you wanna smoke some pot?" Richard knew he had a better shot at feeling her up if Kara was high.

"Sure. I guess," said Kara as he lit a joint and passed it to her. The two traded the smoke back and forth while making small talk.

Richard had a lot of pain in his life. His parents divorced when he was young; his father took out his pain on Richard. Richard was able to let down his guard only to Kara. Because they had been friends for so long, it was easier for him to share his feelings. Now that they were getting older and able to smoke or have a drink together, it only made the bond tighter. He knew they had a close friendship and even though he thought she was kind of cute, he wasn't really interested in anything more than a friend and an occasional make-out buddy. Kara, unfortunately mistook his attention for far more. She would become jealous when he talked to other girls in the neighborhood. He could tell how she felt, but he knew there would be a back lash if he denied blatantly his lack of interest. When Kara feelings got hurt the world paid.

Richard looked handsome, freshly showered and his thick brown hair slicked back. He wore Levis as if they made the pants just for him. They took turns stretching their hands back and forth, passing the joint. Richard looked at Kara in the moonlight; *well she's not too bad.* Kara was laying it on thick, laughing at everything he said and hanging on his every word, listening for a change instead of running her mouth to impress him.

She was sitting on the bottom of the slide and he was at the top. Suddenly, Richard slid down, bumping into Kara. She didn't move and he ended up with his legs straddling her body. They started making out. Kara knew she was high and started to get a little worried. She knew she shouldn't be doing this while she was supposed to be watching someone's kids.

"Hey, let's go inside so we can hear the children if they wake up," Kara said, ignoring Ms. Rodgers rule about no company.

"Sure," Richard shrugged.

They went inside and both took of their shoes, tip-toeing up the steps. Kara led him into the living room—the room that was off limits for everyone, including the Rodgers kids. She grabbed two sodas out of the kitchen and the two had a seat on the floral-print couch. Before he could make his move, Kara made hers. Grabbing his hand and putting it on her waist. They began to make out. Kara pushed Richard back onto the arm of the sofa and tried to make her way on top of him. Richard's high was wearing off and the reality of what was happening turned him off. He suddenly pushed her off of him.

"What's wrong?" said Kara, realizing she had behaved too desperately. Ever the manipulator, she pretended her feelings were hurt as she dropped her head and tried to force tears. Kara's eyes began to water.

Richard took her hands. "Let's just slow down." Then he gently eased Kara back on the sofa and kissed her.

He was fine with just kissing Kara when they both were sitting up, with him slightly easing her back for a more comfortable position on the sofa. Then Kara put her feet all the way up on the sofa and slid down hoping that Richard would follow her lead.

"I gotta go," said Richard, having seen enough. He was totally uncomfortable with the way Kara was acting and had no desire whatsoever to stick around any longer.

The following day Ms. Rodgers got the full report from her daughter. She called Kara's mom to inform her Kara was fired. Of course Kara didn't suffer any consequences for her actions. She just blamed it all on Richard. Sherry didn't hear about the events until Ms. Rodgers specifically told her no guests, but especially "no Kara."

Kara thought about seeing Richard on the other side of the river and was undecided.

"Go ahead Kara," said Sherry, knowing that's what she really wanted anyways. "I'll go check on Larence and catch up with you."

Sherry was thinking positively and hoping that nothing would be wrong when she got over to see the younger kids. She didn't have to tell Kara twice. She and Bernadette skated off without a second thought.

Once again, Sherry was disappointed in Kara. But because she had come to expect nothing more from her, it didn't sting so badly. She took off heading toward the beach hoping to reach her brother. She was moving as fast as her sneakers could carry her on the ice, staying close to the riverbank.

Iceburg

From behind her, she heard someone saying, "Wait up!" Sherry glanced back and saw Bernadette. She was a better friend than Kara could ever be. Up until the time Kara moved into the neighborhood, Bernadette and Sherry were best friends. Sherry thought back on how she met Kara and how quickly they became inseparable. Contrasted with how she was feeling now, she thought maybe the friendship had simply been outgrown.

As Sherry got closer to the beach front, the ice was softer and water started to seep into her tennis shoes. For once, Sherry was grateful that her mother always made her put plastic bags between her socks and shoes when there was snow on the ground. She came up on the beach and could see Larence on the ice.

"Larence!" she screamed. He couldn't swim and *knew* better than to be on the ice. *Lord, please let me get to him in time,* Sherry thought, seeing her dream come true before her eyes.

"I'm cold, Sherry," Larence hollered back to her.

She was getting closer and shouted, "Get back on the beach!"

Larence looked scared. "I can't!"

Sherry looked at him and noticed he was standing on a floating chunk of ice. She didn't know how it happened and didn't have time to discuss it. She saw the other kids around, standing on similar ice chunks, some of them pushing themselves around with long sticks, like it was some kind of game.

What the hell is wrong with these little monsters, Sherry wondered. It amazed her that in their collective brain power, no one thought this was a stupid idea. The red-headed Calaverie twins were there, dressed alike despite being a little too old to still be wearing identical outfits. She wasn't surprised to see them floating around, both boys were all brawn and no brains. She also saw the owl-eyed Whittnore trio, Karl, Alison and Mark. They were the brainiacs of school; they all got very good grades and were seldom in trouble. It was rare to see them without their mother over their shoulder and Sherry was shocked to see them in on the icy action. They were smart, but not without their own issues. Sherry had seen Mark tell a bold-faced lie before without so much as flinching. He had been sledding with the other kids last winter on the other side of Rodgers Hill, past the one block radius his mother had permitted him. When she asked about the injury he sustained while sledding, he lied and said Sherry Sweetstone had pushed him down. Sherry was not even out that day; she was babysitting. And that's just what she had Miss Jasmine tell Mrs. Whittnore, that Sherry was watching her children. The Whittnores didn't apparently know Sherry's reputation. All the other families knew she was responsible, why else would they entrust their children with her.

Sherry saw James Barnes was there too. He snickered at Larence's dilemma. Everyone seemed to be having fun but Larence. That was only because he was the only one smart enough to realize the predicament he was in, being unable to swim and surrounded by water. James thought everything was funny, though, and it didn't surprise her at all to see him laugh. Most of the time, he was completely clueless when things got serious.

"Ok Larence, let's get you in," said Sherry calmly. "How long have you been out here?"

"I don't know. Maybe an hour and a half," said Larence.

She shook her head. She never knew what it was that made kids, including herself, feel like they needed to prove something to one another.

"Do you want me to hold your hand?"

Larence looked around at the other children who were snickering. "No," he said coolly.

Sherry had a gut feeling that she needed to grab his hand, but brushed it off when she saw him get embarrassed. "Ok fine. Just follow me."

She jumped two feet to a broken iceberg. "Come on Larence, you can do it".

He followed her, though it took him a moment to get up the courage.

She jumped again. Larence followed safely.

The third jump was much wider than the first too. Though Larence was a good athlete, he was still pretty small. He watched as Sherry jumped. She once again shook off the urge to grab his hand, turning back to

Iceburg

encourage him. Knowing this was the last big jump he had to make and the quickest path to shore, he knew he had to make it.

Larence gave it all he had, but knew mid-jump that it wouldn't be enough. His foot touched the edge of the chunk he was leaping too, but the edge of an ice slab isn't sturdy. Sherry watched as his face changed to panic and he slipped beneath the surface of the water.

His hands grabbed the ice, and his head rose up, gasping for air. The ice was slippery and he couldn't maintain a grip. Soon the water overtook his head and though he was flailing his arms and legs, assuming he could at least get his head above water, he sunk like a rock. It wasn't that deep, but deep enough to cover him. His feet hit the surface below. The water was freezing and it took no time for it to begin aching, his toes and fingers going numb almost instantly. He held his breath. Larence tried to stand up on his tiptoes, thinking it would make him taller and possibly close enough to the surface. He waved his hands over his head and could reach the air, but his body wouldn't follow.

Not thinking about the freezing water, Sherry laid across the large piece of ice, reached in and grabbed Laurence's wrists. With everything she had Sherry pulled Larence out of the Severn River. He was twice his weight with the water weighing his clothes down and Sherry wasn't sure how she managed to lift him. But he was alive. Dripping wet and cold as ice, but alive.

"You alright Larence?" Sherry shook him and rubbed his face briskly.

Larence nodded his head and she brought him close, putting her arms around him tightly. This time she was not letting him go. Sherry looked around for help. It all happened so fast that no one seemed to have noticed. Sherry knew that if she wasn't there, none of the other kids would have seen Larence fall. They wouldn't have saved him. Sherry was angry. These kids were supposed to be friends, to look out for one another. Suddenly she realized they all were grasping the severity of what had happened. There was concern in their eyes as if they wanted to help. But at this point, Sherry didn't trust anyone with the safety of Larence. She and her little brother jumped from one Iceburg to another together until they finally reached shore.

Then, after they were safe and her heart rate had slowed a little, Sherry remembered her dream. She remembered she needed to keep him moving and warm. Sherry walked Larence quickly to the edge of the beach where there were no distractions and no chances of falling back in the water. She ripped off Laurence's coat and put hers on him, just like she had done in her dream. Her coat was long, lined with corduroy and filled with down. It wasn't the cutest thing, but she was convinced that cute wasn't what God had in mind when he directed her hand to choosing this coat from the closet. It went past Larence's knees, almost to his ankles. Larence immediately began warming up. She thought about how much trouble they would be in if their parents saw Larence soaking wet. Instead of being grateful that he was okay, they would instead dwell on the fact that things could have been much worse. They were caught up in their own fears of not being good-enough parents to appreciate that their only daughter had saved their youngest son's life. Instead, they would wonder who was there and who saw the incident. She thought it might be best to have him dry off at a friend's but her gut told her get him home.

"What do you want to do Larence?" Sherry was scared but didn't want to show it. She knew he would understand the risks involved with going straight home.

"Sherry, I want to go home," Larence said fighting back the tears.

"It's okay Larence. Nothing is going to happen to you; I'll get you home."

She grabbed her brother and put her arms around him. She managed to fit them both in the coat. With her right arm in the right sleeve, and his in the left, they began the long walk home.

As they walked, Sherry realized she had been guided by God through her dream. She felt special and grateful. As they got closer to the driveway, she told Larence to sneak into the house so as not to make a commotion, and to get out of his wet clothes.

The day had been exhausting, but it had also been a culmination of many things in Sherry's life. Her dreams were serving as warnings; there was no denying it anymore. She knew now to trust herself and God and that she wouldn't be led astray. She didn't feel like a hero, but a part of her knew that her brother may have drowned without her.

Also, the day confirmed to Sherry that it was time to let one particular old friendship die out. It had been a long time coming, and although she wouldn't abandon Kara completely, she knew the friendship would never be even remotely the same.

Chapter 7
The Cul-de-sac

The air was hot and humid, a typical summer day in River Sades. July was one of Sherry's favorite months because school was out and Independence Day was quite possibly the best holiday ever. Bernadette and Sherry had rekindled their friendship over an hour-long telephone conversation. It would've gone on longer if Bernadette hadn't just invited her over. Sherry looked forward to hanging out with a normal girl again, one that didn't think that anything not involving the potential for trouble was boring. She arrived at Bernadette's house within minutes.

She felt a peace that she hadn't felt in a long time ringing Bernadette's door bell. She realized she should have trusted her gut; all those years ringing Kara's doorbell she felt anxious, almost sick to her stomach. But, she was learning. Ms. Rodgers had told her that sometimes even grownups forgot to follow their intuition. While Sherry figured she was on the right path, listening to her dreams and recognizing that "gut feeling", it was reassuring to know that she had plenty of time to perfect it. That moment, standing at Bernadette's door, she said a little prayer. *God, I know I don't always listen when you try to speak to me. But I'm trying. And I really hope that counts for something.*

Bernadette answered the door smiling, with her sneakers on and two sodas in hand.

"Hey let's go up the street to the cul-de-sac, it's too nice to be inside." She handed Sherry a can and the two began walking.

Iceburg

Near the center of River Sades was a cul-de-sac where the kids would congregate to play. It wasn't what you traditionally thought of as a cul-de-sac, with driveways spilling into it. Instead, it was a giant empty field. No one knew why it was called the cul-de-sac, and really no one questioned it.

"Wow!" said Sherry as they approached. "Everyone and their grandmother is here!"

Sherry noticed Larence and Maurice were wrapping up a serious game of kick ball with about every other boy in the neighborhood.

"We are in next game!" shouted Bernadette, smiling to Sherry.

You had to be a great ball player to be a girl picked on the teams with the guys from the neighborhood. Sherry and Bernadette were among the few girls that they let play with them because they both had brothers who taught them well. Sherry thought of Kara and realized why she never likes being at the Cul de Sac. For one, she wouldn't get the attention she craved because everyone was distracted with real fun, and also because Bernadette was well-received here. Not to mention, Kara was not good at ball sports. And that was one thing Sherry and Bernadette had in common. Sherry was glad Kara wasn't here; now she didn't have the pressure of Kara making rude comments on the side line like. She could imagine her now...*when is the game going to be over!? I'm so bored; I can't believe you like this Sherry.* Sherry immediately tried to push the negative thoughts out of her mind. She was determined to move on from Kara's overbearing ways and general bad attitude. She was too young to be bogged down by another person's issues.

"Alright, you girls are team captains!" shouted Maurice, snapping Sherry back to the scene at hand.

They ran to the top of the field. The coin was tossed by James Barnes, "Call it!"

"Heads," said Sherry.

"Heads wins," said James smiling widely at her. "You pick first." Sherry wasn't sure if the smile was a flirt or an effort to get her to pick him.

But, she smiled back and said, "I choose you."

The teams were pretty even, and Bernadette ended up with the Sweetstone boys on her side.

The sun beamed down extra hot that day as the kids played their hardest and their fastest. It felt like it was the last kick ball game of their lives the way they all had their heads in the game. They played seven innings that day, with Larence making the final play.

The bases were loaded. Larence kicked the ball way out into left field. As Vincent chased after it, three runners crossed home plate, tying the score before the ball made it back home. Sherry was manning home plate and she knew she had to get Larence out to stop them from winning. Seeing him rounding third she thought of how lucky she was to be able to see him run and play, to have not lost him to the icy river that day. Suddenly Sherry looked center field just in time to see the ball headed right for her. It bounced off her chest, stinging as it hit, and she ran to catch up with it again. She grabbed the ball and ran to intersect Larence. She hated to do it to her little brother, but it was part of the game. Sherry stood along the base line and threw directly at his midsection. She threw hard. Out of nowhere Larence jumped up, doing the splits at about four feet off the ground. He landed and took two giant strides to home, winning the game.

Both Sherry and Larence were smiling from ear to ear when he turned around. She went to give him a high five and the two grasped hands. They shared a glance that said everything; that they were forever bonded and would forever be sharing in each other's victories.

THE END